"What's an elephant say? Do you know?"

Landon's daughter squeezed the elephant with both hands then shoved one of its floppy ears in her mouth.

Boy, if his buddies from the bull-riding circuit could see him now, they'd be doubled over with laughter. But he didn't care because he'd do anything to make his baby girl happy.

After a few failed attempts and not a little struggling, he finally got her diaper changed and he even managed to put on a clean white T-shirt and a gray pair of pants. At least he was helping. That should count for something.

Holding Adeline carefully in his arms, he walked back out to the kitchen. The aroma of something delicious baking made his mouth water.

"This casserole is huge." Kelsey gestured toward the oven with her thumb. "Do you want to stay for dinner?"

Yes. No. "Sure, why not?"

Accepting her invitation meant a homecooked meal and more time with Adeline. A win-win. But spending an evening with Kelsey was dicey and only reminded him of what he couldn't have—Adeline and Kelsey in his life.

Together.

Heidi McCahan is a Pacific Northwest girl at heart, but now resides in North Carolina with her husband and three boys. When she isn't writing inspirational romance novels, Heidi can usually be found reading a book, enjoying a cup of coffee and avoiding the laundry pile. She's also a huge fan of dark chocolate and her adorable goldendoodle, Finn. She enjoys connecting with readers, so please visit her website, heidimccahan.com.

Books by Heidi McCahan

Love Inspired

The Firefighter's Twins
Their Baby Blessing
An Unexpected Arrangement
The Bull Rider's Fresh Start

Visit the Author Profile page at Harlequin.com.

The Bull Rider's Fresh Start

Heidi McCahan

LOVE INSPIRED
INSPIRATIONAL ROMANCE

LOVE INSPIRED®
INSPIRATIONAL ROMANCE

Recycling programs
for this product may
not exist in your area.

ISBN-13: 978-1-335-75878-1

The Bull Rider's Fresh Start

Copyright © 2021 by Heidi Blankenship

This edition published by arrangement with Harlequin Books S.A.

For questions and comments about the quality of this book, please contact us
at CustomerService@Harlequin.com.

Love Inspired
22 Adelaide St. West, 40th Floor
Toronto, Ontario M5H 4E3, Canada
www.Harlequin.com

Printed in U.S.A.

Behold, I will do a new thing; now it shall spring forth; shall ye not know it? I will even make a way in the wilderness, and rivers in the desert.
—*Isaiah* 43:19

For my mom, who has taught us
how to love well in hard seasons.

Chapter One

He'd clung to the backs of enraged bulls for thousands of wild rides. In his tireless pursuit of world champion status, he'd endured a punctured lung, broken bones and more torn ligaments than he cared to recall.

But never once had a crying baby threatened to bring him to his knees.

Landon Chambers palmed the back of his neck and stared at the wailing baby girl buckled in the car seat in the middle of his grandparents' living room floor.

Physical therapy for his nagging back injury? All over it. Sobriety? Two hundred seventy days and counting. Working as a third-generation wheat farmer? He'd make it work or die trying.

But caring for a baby? Not so much.

This ancient farmhouse he'd inherited when his grandparents moved to an assisted living facility earlier this year wasn't a suitable place for a nine-month-old baby.

He never should've agreed to this.

Landon stifled a groan. When his best friend Wade called and announced he and his wife, Maggie, were temporary caregivers for Adeline, the infant of a deployed single mom, he hadn't given the news much thought. He'd admittedly been a little absorbed with his own life and hadn't bothered to ask many questions. Or any questions at all, to be honest. Seemed like a selfless move, which was typical of Wade. He'd always been generous, even at the height of his successful professional bull riding career. It wasn't like Landon had expected Wade and his wife to go and die on him. The unfairness of it all stole Landon's breath worse than a Brahma flinging him into the dirt.

"Adeline, I have no idea what I'm supposed to do with you. Any suggestions?"

She stopped crying as if she might answer him, but she only sucked in a breath, then started screaming again. He had zero experience with babies, but even he knew she couldn't speak yet. Instead her wide blue eyes bored into him and her cheeks flushed a deeper shade of pink while she kicked her bare feet against the car seat's gray padding. Landon unbuttoned the cuffs of his white button-down and rolled up the sleeves.

"Hold on, pretty girl." Landon sank onto the area rug and fumbled with the plastic and metal buckles. He'd encountered gates on cattle chutes less complicated than these things. Finally, he released the contraption and pressed her little body to his shoulder. Her scalp was warm against his chin, and her yellow onesie felt damp under his palm.

"Wow, you are all worked up."

She arched her back and wailed louder, as if this new arrangement didn't suit her, either.

Oh man. Babies needed instruction manuals.

When he'd visited Wade's father and stepmother's house in Wyoming yesterday, he'd never imagined he'd be returning home with a baby. Wade's stepmother had all but begged him to take Adeline. He must've been her only option because he was the last guy who should be responsible for a kid. If it weren't for the desperate panic in the older woman's eyes, he might've laughed at her request. She'd insisted that she couldn't care for her husband and a demanding infant, too. At first, Landon had refused, but their grief inundated every corner of the comfortable ranch-style home. One look at Wade's father's condition forced Landon to reconsider. Besides, Wade's stepmother promised the situation was temporary. As soon as the baby's mother came home from overseas, he'd be able to hand Adeline over.

So he'd said yes. Then patiently listened to the instructions offered and scanned the notes scribbled on a notepad, but he'd only absorbed about half of the information. The whole scenario felt surreal. He'd quickly read the notes again when he got home last night. There weren't any tips for soothing Adeline's sorrow.

Poor thing. He'd lost two of his dearest friends, but she'd lost the people who'd loved and cared for her. Everything about her world had turned upside down. No wonder she cried so much. It was probably her only coping strategy.

"All right, sweetie." He patted her backside as he moved slowly around the living room, his cowboy boots clicking across the hardwood. "Stick with me. We'll figure this out."

Taking her to church with him this morning had seemed like a good idea at the time. The volunteers in the nursery knew how to keep her safe, so he didn't feel guilty about leaving her for an hour or so. It was time he desperately needed to chase down answers to the questions swirling in his head, like an angry bull circling the arena, desperate for a way out.

How was he supposed to take care of a baby and work on his parents' farm? They had hundreds of acres of wheat to harvest in the next ten days. While Wade's stepmother had insisted he was the best person to care for Adeline, Landon's doubts had resurfaced on the long drive back to his house in Colorado. He was a recovering addict with a mountain of debt. Wheat harvest meant long hours in the field, driving the combine and the trucks. They might even work through the night to get the wheat in and avoid a forecasted storm. If Adeline's mother didn't come home soon, he didn't have the foggiest idea how he'd find a babysitter.

What had he done?

He still couldn't believe a drunk driver had recklessly snuffed out Wade and Maggie's lives while they drove home from a concert in Denver last week. His throat tightened at the thought of the accident.

Adeline ramped up her crying to a deafening pitch. Was there anything worse than a helpless infant in distress? No time to dwell on all they'd lost. He had to stop the crying.

Landon had a room full of trophies and awards from his reign as a world-champion bull rider. But an angry, two-thousand-pound bull was far less terrifying than a crying baby. A bull bucked him off in eight seconds or less, then they went their separate ways. When things went wrong, a clown or a handler bailed him out.

But this time there wasn't anyone coming to his rescue. At least not right away. His parents lived on the farm close by, and they'd handled the news about Adeline moving in with a mixture of sadness and encouragement. They'd known Wade, too. Everyone who'd known Wade and Maggie grieved their loss. While he couldn't return Adeline or undo the accident that had taken her caregivers away, some small part of him still hoped this was all a horrible nightmare. He couldn't fathom how he'd juggle real life and caring for Adeline.

"It's going to be okay," he whispered against her soft brown hair. A statement meant for his own peace of mind, anyway. She didn't seem real interested in what he had to say. Landon moved toward the kitchen where he'd left his wallet, phone and Adeline's diaper bag. Her crying softened a little, boosting his confidence. The volunteers in the nursery had assured him some babies liked motion. Maybe walking helped.

Holding her carefully, he stopped moving and unzipped the canvas bag on the counter. The sweet fragrance he'd come to associate with all things baby greeted him as he pushed past the diapers, package of wipes and extra change of clothes tucked in the main compartment. Thankfully, Wade's stepmother had packed for him before he'd left yesterday. He had no idea what kind of supplies he needed, or that he even needed to haul around a bag like this. He had a lot to learn.

Including why this bag housed so many pockets but he still couldn't find what he needed. Surely there was a pacifier in here somewhere. Babies liked those, right? Hopefully Adeline was a fan.

She amped up her crying again. Maybe because he'd stopped moving? Finally, he found a pacifier in the last mesh pocket.

"Look what I have." He tried to keep his voice calm. What if she hated it? He turned her around and braced her back against his chest, then offered the pacifier. She swiveled her head away.

"Come on, Adeline." He gently tapped her lower lip with the pink and white pacifier. This time she batted his hand away with her own and screamed louder.

"Message delivered." He pushed out a sigh. She arched her back and wailed some more. Landon set the pacifier on the counter and glanced at his phone. At what point did he call for backup? His parents had promised they'd help, although they'd gone out for lunch with friends in Limon after church. They probably weren't home yet. Laramie and Jack, his sister and brother-in-law, had twins. Laramie had worked as a nanny in college, so she'd know exactly what to do. She was also six months pregnant, so he hated to ask her to rescue him.

He had to find a way to comfort Adeline. Did it hurt a baby to cry this much?

They'd fed her a bottle and changed her diaper while she'd stayed in the church nursery. Was he supposed to feed her again? Did she eat regular food? He'd spooned a few bites of baby oatmeal into her mouth this morning, just like Wade's stepmother said he should. More of the sticky concoction landed on her clothes than in her mouth, but at least he'd tried. Add feeding a baby properly to the long list of things he needed to learn. And fast.

Defeated, he reached for his phone and sent Laramie a quick text. He wasn't too proud to admit he desperately needed help.

* * *

Nothing was going to get between Kelsey and her baby.

A clap of thunder overhead made her yelp, followed quickly by a bolt of lightning that sizzled from the ominous purple sky to the wet highway in front of her.

"You're not slowing me down," Kelsey growled at the storm pelting her rented car with blinding sheets of rain. She blinked away the grit of fatigue in her eyes and forced herself to concentrate on the interstate. Despite her fierce determination to be with her daughter, every leg of her marathon journey to Colorado had been an uphill battle.

The horrible news of her stepbrother and sister-in-law's deaths had taken an extra day to reach her since the navy had assigned her to a dive off a remote island in the South Pacific. Then her commanding officer took longer than expected to approve her leave. By the time she got to shore, she'd missed her flight to Honolulu. After waiting another sixteen hours, she'd begged and cajoled her way into the last available seat. More than three days had passed before she reached California. When her plane took off for Denver, she could barely move from sheer exhaustion.

Finally, she was less than an hour away from seeing her daughter. Her heart thrummed with anticipation. The occasional video call and dozens of photos Wade had sent her while she was deployed served as a poor substitute for holding her child in her arms. But she'd done what she thought was best—leaving Adeline with Wade and Maggie on their Wyoming ranch while she fulfilled her commitment to the navy. They'd grudgingly promised to conceal the baby's paternity.

So much for that plan. Kelsey had sobbed over the loss of her stepbrother and his amazing wife. She'd grieved all the ways their absence impacted her baby girl. And she'd cried about what this new reality meant for her. Because she'd get to see Adeline soon, but she'd also have to face the one person she never wanted to see again—Adeline's father.

She was probably supposed to be grateful, since Adeline was technically with her biological father. Except the man was addicted to pain meds and had no business caring for anyone, especially her child. When her mother had called last night to say they'd sent Adeline to Colorado with Landon, Kelsey wanted to scream. They knew all about Landon's issues. She couldn't believe her stepfather didn't think about that before they handed a helpless infant over to the most irresponsible man on the planet. They must've been overwhelmed with grief and unable to think clearly, because that was the only explanation Kelsey could come up with to justify such a careless decision.

Allowing Landon anywhere near Adeline was never part of their agreement. They'd even signed the paperwork and she'd submitted the plan to her commanding officer to comply with the military's requirements for single mothers.

Anger burned raw and hot inside and she squeezed the steering wheel tighter. The rain pummeled her car, drowning out the country music playing on the radio as the storm rolled over the wide, open prairie of eastern Colorado. Reluctantly, Kelsey let up on the gas pedal and slowed down. She had to stay safe for Adeline's sake. Stealing a glance at the app on her phone, she double-checked the directions. Four more miles to the exit. At least the drive from the Denver airport to Landon's place was less than two hours. Every part of her body ached with fatigue from traveling for so long. Or maybe her emotional distress fueled her weariness, in addition to the grueling trip. She couldn't wait to see her baby again but loathed the thought of speaking with Landon.

Like the water tracing a path across her driver's side window, a rivulet of guilt worked its way into her heart. *Concealing the truth from him isn't right.* Kelsey shook her head, dismissing the persistent thought that had dogged her all the way across the Pacific. She'd started attending church and a Bible study as often as she could and had given her heart to the Lord a few months back. The verses didn't always make sense, but she'd read and understood enough to know that lying wasn't okay.

He deserves to know he's Adeline's father.

"He doesn't deserve anything," she protested, then jabbed at a button on the steering wheel to turn up the volume on the radio.

While she sang along to the familiar lyrics of a country megastar's latest hit, more questions about Landon spooled through her mind. Did Wade and Maggie go back on their word and tell him Adeline was his daughter before they died? Or maybe her mother had spilled the truth, and that's how she'd persuaded him to take Adeline? And why didn't they ask her before they made this decision? Maybe this crazy arrangement wasn't even legal. She made a mental note to call an attorney.

Thoughts of Landon invaded next. She'd tried so hard not to think about him, but she was minutes away from showing up at his door. No matter how determined she was to protect Adeline, she didn't trust herself to be impervious to his charms.

They'd met at Wade and Maggie's wedding. She'd known he was trouble from the second their gazes locked during the rehearsal. And yet he'd sweet-talked his way right past her defenses. Warmth heated her skin at the memory of his smile, those cavernous dimples and the way he made her feel like she was the only woman in the room.

She'd avoided him until the reception, sidestepping all his attempts at conversation. He wouldn't give up. She agreed to dance one time, hoping he'd finally leave her alone. Except he spun her around the reception hall like he was made to two-step. And the way he looked in that black tuxedo stole her breath. One song led to two and then three. Then she found herself outside under the vast Wyoming sky, sipping punch with Landon. A moonlight kiss quickly accelerated into a passionate night together.

Waking up alone shouldn't have surprised her. Landon's reputation wasn't a secret. But the heartache—there wasn't a remedy for the emotional pain his absence left. Except hard work. She was a navy diver, a job that required every ounce of strength and stamina she possessed. When the pregnancy test turned out to be positive, she'd vowed not to tell him. She'd made a terrible mistake. Telling a man like Landon Chambers he was going to be a father only jeopardized her baby's future. She should know; she'd lived with an addict for much of her childhood. Landon only cared about himself, so how could she possibly trust him with the responsibility of parenthood?

Wade had told her plenty of stories. How Landon ruined his bull riding career with his addiction to pills. He was an addict, and addicts rarely changed. Her own father's fatal overdose had taught her that. That's why she had to get Adeline away from Landon.

He wasn't single-dad material. He was wild and out of control. More like a shameless party animal who belonged with the bulls he rode.

Red lights on the back of a giant tractor-trailer suddenly appeared in front of her, and Kelsey stomped on the brakes. See? Even thinking about Landon got her into trouble. The truck crept along the interstate, and Kelsey drew a few deep breaths to ease her frazzled nerves.

Her phone directed her to take the next exit for Merritt's Crossing. The truck in front of her led the way, its signal a blinking red beacon in the rain-soaked afternoon as they eased off the interstate. At the top of the ramp, the truck turned left toward a motel, fast food restaurants, a gas station and a convenience store.

Kelsey hesitated. Maybe she should rent a motel room. Then she'd have someplace to bring Adeline once she picked her up from Landon's house. *No.* Every minute her baby spent with him was one minute too many. She'd navigated sleep deprivation many times in her military career and was trained to withstand physical exhaustion. She could do this.

Instead of following the truck, she obeyed the directions and turned right. As she left the lights from the gas station in her rearview mirror and traveled between wheat fields on a two-lane dirt road, her palms turned clammy.

Oh, what a mess. If Landon had figured out Adeline was his, she'd have to explain why she'd never told him.

And if he didn't know, well, she was supposed to confess the truth. Right? But what if he tried to keep Adeline? Dread dived straight through her.

She wouldn't let that happen.

Releasing a frustrated groan, she leaned forward, struggling to navigate the narrow road in the driving rain. If only Maggie and Wade were still alive. Then she wouldn't be trapped in this impossible situation. Her daughter would have a safe, stable home.

Maggie and Wade were good people. Why did this have to happen?

She turned onto yet another narrow, unpaved road flanked by wheat and corn fields. Lightning flashed in front of her, and she rubbed at the tension knotting the muscles in her shoulders. Only a few more minutes. Then she'd be able to hold her baby girl again. Tears pricked at her eyelids. She'd been away for far too long.

The bossy voice on her phone told her to turn right. She complied, but not before her mirror clipped the mailbox.

Oh no. She winced and tried to assess the damage, which was next to impossible given the storm. Didn't anyone around here believe in extra lighting to illuminate their driveways? She might've grown up in Oklahoma, but she and farms never did get along. Ranch life wasn't her thing, either. That's why she loved serving as a diver in the navy. All her needs were met, and she had the opportunity to see the world. As soon as she finished her commitment, she'd further her education and get a great job as a nurse. The kind of job that would provide the childhood for Adeline that she'd never had.

The driveway ended in front of a two-story white farmhouse with black shutters. An adorable swing hung at the far end of the wraparound porch. Was this it? Her pulse sped as she parked and turned off the ignition. Grabbing her purse, she hopped out of the car and promptly stepped in a mud puddle.

Great. Slinging her purse strap over her shoulder, she jogged across the yard, her flip-flops slapping against her heels. She hesitated at the bottom of the porch's wide steps, her mouth as dry as cotton. What if this was a horrible mistake?

Thoughts of seeing Adeline propelled her up the steps, and she knocked on the door. It swung open, revealing Landon looking more handsome than she remembered in a crisp white button-down and dark denim jeans.

"I hope you brought more di…" Landon's deep voice trailed off as recognition flashed in his hazel eyes. Thunder rumbled overhead. "Kelsey? What are you doing here?"

"I'm here for Adeline."

He studied her russet-brown hair piled in a messy bun and those full pink lips flattened in a thin line. Daring him to challenge her. The weight of her amber gaze leveled him. She wasn't kidding. When he'd hoped for a rescuer, the woman he'd spent one night with eighteen months ago and never called again hadn't been the first person he'd anticipated.

"Where is she?" In the doorway of his farmhouse, Kelsey pushed up on her toes and craned her neck, obviously scanning the room behind him. Creases formed in her smooth brow like a tiny number eleven, broadcasting her concern.

He let his gaze quickly travel from her pale blue

T-shirt to her dark jeans, stylishly cuffed above her ankles, and brown flip-flops. No nail polish on her tanned toes. She twined her fingers around the strap of her brown leather purse. That furrow between her brows said she wasn't thrilled to see him. He couldn't blame her. Yet all these months later, her stunning beauty captivated him.

"Adeline's asleep." *Finally.* He clutched the edge of the thick old door. He owed his friend Gage a cheeseburger and a milkshake for sharing his secret sauce for getting a baby to stop crying.

Kelsey glared at the fancy watch on her slender wrist. Evidently, this news impacted her itinerary. He rubbed his fingers along his jaw, trying to piece together exactly how she'd arrived on his doorstep. Did she think she could drop by unannounced and make ridiculous demands? The intensity in her expression hinted at something more. He owed her an explanation. An apology. At the very least some decent manners. She'd just lost two people she loved also.

Landon stepped back and pulled the door open. "This weather is nasty. Would you like to come in for a few minutes?"

She paused on the threshold as though this was truly a life-changing decision. Then she tucked a loose strand of her hair behind her ear and nodded.

He held his breath as she moved into the foyer of his grandparents' home. A subtle fragrance drifted into the narrow space. Lavender. Must be her soap or shampoo. It rocketed him back in time to Wade and Maggie's wedding and the night they'd spent together.

Landon cleared his throat. "Kelsey, I—"

"Don't." Her purse slid to the floor and hit the hardwood with a *thunk*, like an exclamation point on the end of her command.

He closed the door and faced her.

"I'm not here to talk about…the past." She tipped her chin up, a muscle in her square jaw knotting as she drilled him with her coffee-colored gaze. "I'm here to collect Adeline and her things, and then I'll be on my way."

Wait. What? Confusion washed through him. He linked his arms across his chest. "What do you mean, you're here to collect Adeline?"

"She's coming with me." She propped her hands on her hips. He tried not to let his eyes wander to the shapely curve of her biceps, or her smooth skin burnished to a tawny brown, hinting at the hours she spent in the sun. Pink clung to her cheekbones, and the ancient light fixture overhead highlighted the red tones in her hair.

Her intensity unnerved him. He wouldn't let her see him sweat, though. "Your mom mentioned you travel for work. I'm sure it's tough keeping up with everything going on back home." He intentionally softened his tone and infused his voice with empathy. "I'm real sorry to hear about Wade and Maggie's accident. And no one was more surprised than me when your mom asked me to take care of Adeline. But I'm a man of my word and—"

Sharp laughter sprung from her lips, interrupting him. "*You're* a man of your word? Well, that's an interesting turn of events, isn't it? Seeing as how you spent the night with me then told me I was better off without you. Don't worry. I didn't lose any sleep waiting for your call."

If sparks could fly from her eyes right now, he'd be pulverized into ashes.

"Not calling you is one of the biggest regrets of my life. I am so sorry."

She stared at him. Her mouth opened then closed. Had his apology taken the fight out of her? Doubtful. But maybe his kind words had bought him thirty seconds to think. "Are you still in the navy?"

"Yes." She surveyed her surroundings—probably mentally forming a list of reasons why a baby couldn't stay here.

"And you're a diver?" He pretended not to know the answers to these questions even though Kelsey's mother had kept up a running commentary the whole time he'd visited. She'd explained the memorial service for Wade and Maggie was on hold until Kelsey's leave was approved and she could come home from Hawaii.

Kelsey nodded, her eyes still scanning the room.

"Do you live on base in military housing when you aren't traveling the world on assignments?"

She huffed out a sigh. "I live on base. Pearl Harbor, Honolulu, Hawaii. For a guy who never wanted to speak to me again, you sure have a lot of questions. What's up with the inquisition?"

Ouch. "I deserve that. Again, I'm sorry for the way I treated you. My decision not to call you was wrong." He paused. Would now be a good time to mention he'd checked himself into inpatient rehab for the second time right after he'd met her? Probably not. She didn't seem real interested in his explanations.

"I'm just wondering how you plan to travel and keep diving with a nine-month-old baby."

"You're something else, you know that?" She scoffed

then blew him off with an impatient wave of her hand. "I'm not having this conversation with you. I don't know why my mother thought this was a good idea. It's not. It's a horrible idea. You're an addict and you have no business caring for a child."

Kelsey's harsh words stung like a bull's horn slamming into his ribs. Wounded, his hackles raised while his patience flagged. She turned away and strode into the living room.

"Where is she?" Kelsey circled the sofa. "I don't care if she's asleep. I'll wake her up, because she's not spending one more minute in this house with you."

Landon stood at least seven inches taller than Kelsey, and he used his height to his advantage. He cut long strides of his own, eating up the distance between her and the laundry room where he'd tucked Adeline away in her car seat. Gage had told him to put her on top of the dryer, but he was terrified she'd somehow flip her car seat and fall off. Instead, he'd turned the dryer on and kept her on the floor, safely buckled in her car seat. She'd fallen asleep about thirty minutes ago. Maybe it wasn't the dryer at all and just sheer exhaustion. Either way, he'd rather endure another broken collarbone than let anyone wake her.

He stepped in front of Kelsey and braced for impact as he blocked her path.

She gasped and pressed her palms against his chest. The hurt that flashed in her eyes knifed at him. Man, he didn't like making her angry.

He gently clasped her upper arms with both hands. The warmth of her skin made him painfully aware of how much he'd missed her.

"I'm sorry if I've upset you." He lowered his voice to

almost a whisper. "Please don't wake her up. I'm begging you. She's cried most of the day. I couldn't get her to settle down after church, and she's been asleep for less than an hour. Why don't you let her finish her nap? I'll fix you something to eat while you wait."

Moisture glistened on the fringes of her dark eyelashes, and she looked away. *Oh no. Please don't cry.* He couldn't handle another person crying today. After what felt like an eternity, she extracted herself from his hold and backtracked toward the living room.

"I don't need any food," she said, stopping in front of the wide front windows. "I'll wait here until she's awake."

With her back to him, she couldn't see his face. Landon silently mouthed a prayer of thanks toward the sky. He rounded the end of his grandmother's upholstered sofa and eased onto one of the brown-and-orange-flowered cushions.

"I don't want to make you angrier, but—"

"Oh, go ahead." Her icy tone dripped with sarcasm. "You're on a roll."

He swallowed back a snide response. *A little help here, Lord.* Leaning forward, Landon rested his elbows on his knees and measured his words carefully. "Adeline is blessed to have someone like you looking out for her. But I have questions, because there's a few pieces of this puzzle missing. I can't let you take her until I get some answers."

Kelsey's shoulders stiffened.

Landon plowed on with his questions. "The last time Wade and I talked, he said they were temporarily caring for Adeline. So what about her biological parents? Your mom was really upset. All she'd tell me was that we're waiting for Adeline's biological mother to show up. Do you know anything about her? Should I have contacted social services?"

She flinched as though he'd pelted her in the backside with a snowball. Then she turned slowly and faced him, her arms wrapped around her torso. The guilt flashing in her eyes was easy to recognize. He'd greeted a similar expression in the mirror every morning for months.

"You don't need to call anyone." She barely choked out the words.

That's why she's here. The thought whipped so quickly through his mind that he almost missed it. Wade and Maggie had married eighteen months ago. Math wasn't his gift, but adding nine plus nine wasn't difficult. And that simple calculation added up to the truth. His heart rate accelerated, pounding against his chest.

"Kelsey." Her name left his mouth in a growl.

She trapped her lower lip behind her teeth.

"Who are Adeline's birth parents?"

Chapter Two

She couldn't lie.

She *wouldn't* lie. But the thought of telling Landon the truth terrified her. What happened when he found out Adeline was hers? And his?

Kelsey fisted her hands at her sides to stop the trembling. "Adeline is mine."

The storm raging in Landon's eyes rivaled the one blowing across the fields outside.

"And who is her father?"

A shiver raked her spine. "You."

He slowly straightened then leaned back against the sofa, every movement controlled. Intentional. She tracked the path of his fingertips as they traveled across his forehead. The weight of her confession hung heavy in the musty air. Landon kept his eyes downcast. Was he praying? Doubtful. He'd never behaved like a man who trusted in God.

Another clap of thunder rumbled overhead. Kelsey stared at him, bracing for harsh words. *Say something. Anything.*

His silence made her mind race. She'd answered his

question honestly. Wasn't she supposed to feel lighter? Relieved? Whoever said the truth set you free had never confessed to concealing a baby's paternity.

Landon's gaze slid to meet hers. "Why didn't you tell me?"

The hurt and confusion marring his handsome features sent her insides into a slow, sickening roll. She drew a deep, calming breath. *He's an addict, remember? Don't let him manipulate you.*

He pushed to his feet and paced the room, stopping in front of the wall of trophies, ribbons and photographs documenting his epic career as a world-champion bull rider.

"If I'd told you I was pregnant, would it have made any difference?"

Landon whirled around and strode toward her, stopping inches away. The masculine scent of his soap or aftershave teased her senses. Red splotches dotted his neck. He rubbed his broad palm against his chest. She refused to look away. Refused to let her long-buried attraction to him undermine her intentions. Refused to think about how those strong hands once held her close. Spun her around the dance floor. Stroked her hair.

"If I'd known, I could've helped. I could've supported you and Adeline from day one. She wouldn't have lived with Wade and Maggie." He didn't raise his voice, yet the raw edge in his tone hinted at his barely controlled anger.

"Wade and Maggie are good people." She squeezed the words past an unexpected lump clogging her throat. "They stepped up when I needed them and took on a huge responsibility."

"But they aren't her parents."

"That doesn't matter," she insisted. "Adeline was safe, and she was loved."

Landon glared at her, his chest rising and falling. "You shouldn't have kept the truth from me, Kelsey. I deserved to know I had a child. Worse, you asked my best friend to lie for you. Why? Why would you do that?"

"Because you didn't give me the option of counting on you." Kelsey wanted to scream. "You left me a note in our hotel room that said you were no good for me. That doesn't sound like someone who's ready to be a father, so don't you dare try to make me feel guilty."

She'd kept the note tucked away in her wallet. It was evidence of Landon's hasty exit from her life and the proof she needed to justify her actions.

He pushed out a long breath. "I already told you I'm sorry I never called. I should have. But holding that against me and asking Wade and Maggie to lie about who my kid belongs to isn't right, either."

His hazel eyes flashed as he pointed out her dishonesty yet again. Her chest tightened like he'd pinched off her oxygen supply. She didn't have the emotional energy to argue with him. She'd learned a long time ago that trying to reason with an addict was pointless. And she didn't have the luxury of time. Adeline's future—her safety—was at stake. The navy had given her sixty days to resolve her childcare issues. While she owed Landon the truth, he wasn't the answer to her problems.

"You're right. Asking my family to keep the truth a secret was wrong. I'm sorry. But to be honest, I didn't think you'd care."

He stopped pacing long enough to shoot her another fiery glare. "Is my name on the birth certificate?"

She hesitated, then slowly nodded. This was so much harder than she'd thought it would be.

"Is that why your mom begged me to take her?"

"Good question." Kelsey shrugged one shoulder. "That wasn't part of the plan."

Landon's gaze narrowed. "And what plan is that?"

So much for getting out of here quickly. She shifted her weight from one foot to the other. "The navy requires that I file a family care plan to ensure Adeline is safe and cared for so I can honor my service commitment."

"So Wade and Maggie were listed as her guardians?"

"Temporary caregivers."

"Are you required to file a backup plan?"

Again, more truth telling. She looked down and smoothed the toe of her flip-flop across the floorboards, stalling. Did she really have to tell him about the paperwork her commanding officers required? The clock on the mantel above the fireplace ticked out the seconds, adding to her unease.

She tipped her chin up and looked him in the eye. "I have to file short- and long-term plans."

"Who else is included in these plans?"

"My mother and stepfather."

Landon tipped his head back and stared at the ceiling. "That explains why your mother called me."

Kelsey's scalp prickled. "What's that supposed to mean?"

He met her gaze. The space between them was taut with unspoken doubts and accusations. "Your parents aren't capable of caring for an infant."

"Why not?"

Landon clamped his mouth closed. Regret flickered in his eyes.

"Tell me, Landon." She stepped toward him. "What's wrong with my folks?"

She didn't know.

The realization wrapped around his chest like a bull rope and cinched tight.

"Landon, please." Her chin wobbled. "I need you to tell me what's going on."

Was it really his place to tell her? "When was the last time you spoke to your mom?"

"Yesterday." Her nostrils flared. "You're scaring me. What happened?"

The fear swimming in her eyes gave him pause. He hated that she'd kept Adeline from him, and he was angry that Wade and Maggie had betrayed him by not telling him he was Adeline's dad. And now they just kept peeling back layers of deception. Why hadn't anyone told Kelsey about her stepfather?

"Your stepdad has had some issues lately."

"What kind of issues?"

He held in a groan. "I— You should probably— Isn't it better if you talk to your mom about this?"

"She's not here. You are. *Tell* me."

"All right, all right." Landon held up his palms. "He had a stroke."

Kelsey's eyes rounded, and she sucked in an audible breath. "When?"

"About six weeks ago."

She shook her head. "No, that can't be. They would've told me."

"I'm sorry," he said quietly. His words fell flat. An apology meant nothing to her. And yet he kept trying.

She pressed her palms to her cheeks, then her gaze darted around the room like a trapped animal seeking escape. He surveyed her reaction, trying to anticipate her next move. Was she going to leave? They hadn't even talked about Adeline yet. She'd probably wake up soon, giving them even more opportunities to argue.

Kelsey turned and moved toward the window. "Why didn't they tell me? I call all the time. I mean, as often as I can."

He wished he knew why. "Maybe they didn't want to upset you."

"That's ridiculous." She dismissed his suggestion, like he knew she would. He swallowed back a response. No need to aggravate her more than he already had.

The news of her stepfather's stroke combined with Wade and Maggie's accident had to be a lot to handle. Part of him wanted to help. To pull her into his arms as she grappled with the reality of her family's struggles.

He squelched that crazy notion and stayed on the sofa. He was the last person who needed to try to comfort her. Not that she'd let him, anyway. He'd better give her space to process. Besides, he had arena-size issues of his own to deal with. Like the fact that the baby asleep in his laundry room was his daughter.

Lord, what have I done? He'd prayed more in the last eight months than he ever had in his life. Kicking his pill habit had brought him to his knees again and again. Somehow, he'd thought he'd won. Didn't all these months of sobriety count as a victory? He'd expected a peaceful yet productive summer, spending time with his family and working on the farm. Finally getting out of debt. Not facing unexpected fatherhood.

"I have to talk to him." Kelsey turned and patted her back pockets, as if searching for her phone. "I need more information."

"I can help." He'd spoken with Wade right after his father's stroke. "What would you like to know?"

Doubt flashed in her eyes. She obviously didn't trust him. Fair enough. He wanted her to at least know her stepfather had a good prognosis, and her mom was doing the best she could caring for him.

"Let me get my phone."

"Kelsey, wait."

She hesitated, halfway to the front hall, probably to grab her purse. She turned back and huffed out an impatient breath. "What?"

"We need a plan." He stood and faced her. "A plan for Adeline."

Her brow furrowed. "I already told you, I'm taking her with me when she wakes up. I'll rent a hotel room in town then leave for Wyoming tom—"

"No." Was she out of her mind? "You don't get to show up on my porch, tell me I'm a father, then take my daughter from me."

"Adeline's not staying here with you."

"And you're not leaving with her." Anger stampeded, hot and fierce, through his gut.

Adeline's muffled cries filtered in and interrupted their argument. Kelsey's eyes locked on his, and this time there was no way he could stop her. She pushed past him and strode toward the laundry room, clearly determined to hold her baby girl.

* * *

The ache to comfort her daughter propelled Kelsey across the living room. She half expected Landon to intercept her. Not happening. Nothing could get between her and her baby. She'd traveled too far and waited way too long to hold Adeline again.

Her heart hammered as she reached the laundry room door, then gently nudged it open. Adeline sat in the car seat on the faded linoleum floor.

"Hey, sweet girl." Adeline's cries mingled with the hum of the dryer. Kelsey sank to her knees in front of the car seat and fumbled with the clasps on the five-point harness.

"You've grown so much." She scanned her wisps of golden-brown hair, swooping into a soft curl across her smooth forehead. A rosy flush formed two circles on her pudgy cheeks, and tears clung to her long dark eyelashes. "Come here."

She gently scooped her baby girl out of the car seat's cocoon and nestled her in her arms. Reunited. Finally. Her vision blurred. She patted Adeline's bare leg with her fingertips, enjoying the smooth feeling of her flawless baby skin. And her scent. She drank it in, filling her lungs. Oh, that sweet fragrance. She'd spent many nights lying in her bed in Hawaii, eyes closed while she mentally tried to recreate the scent in her imagination.

Adeline stopped crying and regarded her with wide blue eyes, then shoved a chubby fist toward her mouth, revealing several teeth.

"Oh my. Look at those teeth." Smiling through her tears, she awkwardly bounced her baby girl in her arms.

Adeline babbled around her fist, and Kelsey chuckled. "C'mon, let's find a clean diaper."

She slowly pushed to her feet, turned and collided with Landon in the laundry room doorway. His fingers quickly steadied her with a gentle clasp on her elbows. Landon's gaze bounced between her face and Adeline cradled in her arms. Something indecipherable flickered in his eyes then vanished. He stepped back, releasing his hold on her, and she pushed out a relieved breath.

His broad shoulders, tan skin and gold-flecked hazel eyes still held the power to sweep her into his orbit. She forced her attention back to her baby girl. She couldn't lose focus. Adeline was all that mattered right now.

"She needs her diaper changed," Kelsey said.

Landon held up a diaper and the plastic package of wipes crinkled in his large hand.

"Oh, good." She nodded as if granting her approval. Adeline fussed and arched her back, reminding Kelsey that she wasn't the same tiny infant she had left in Wade and Maggie's care five months ago. She shifted from one foot to the other, quickly adjusting to holding a larger baby determined to squirm out of her grasp. The heat of Landon's expectant gaze warmed her face, and she silently willed him to move out of her way.

She'd changed lots of Adeline's diapers in the eighteen weeks they'd spent together while her daughter was a newborn. But everything about that compliant infant had disappeared. Kelsey scanned her baby's features, memorizing as many details as possible. Adeline's porcelain skin, the slope of her adorable button nose and even the rolls and creases on her legs made Kelsey proud. Such a perfect little human.

"I've made a place to change diapers in the guest room." Landon's deep voice interrupted her thoughts. "If you follow me, I'll show you."

She trailed after him, his brown cowboy boots click-clacking on the worn hardwood floors as they strode down a narrow hallway. The walls on either side were covered in more framed photographs—black-and-white pictures mingled with sepia-toned images documenting his family's long history on their eastern Colorado farm. Kelsey glanced down at Adeline cradled in her arms and savored the sensation of holding her baby close again. Besides, the more she stared at Adeline, the less she noticed the way Landon's crisp white shirt emphasized his muscular frame.

Stop, she mentally scolded. *He's not right for you. Not right for Adeline, either. You've got to get out of here.*

Landon stepped inside a bedroom at the end of the hall. A queen-size bed adorned with a beautiful patchwork quilt filled most of the small room. Framed artwork of a sunset over a golden field of wheat hung on the wall opposite the bed. A portable crib claimed the extra floor space. Landon had layered several towels on top of an old chest of drawers in the far corner. Wipes and diapers, cans of formula, and stacks of baby clothes sat in various piles on the floor beside the bed.

"I've changed her on top of the dresser a few times."

"But that's dangerous," Kelsey protested. "What if she rolls off?"

A muscle in Landon's jaw flexed. "Feel free to change her wherever you'd like. She's probably hungry. I'll get started fixing a bottle." He tossed the diaper and wipes on the bed then brushed past her and left the room, an appealing aroma of leather and spice lingering behind him.

Adeline cried louder. Her face flushed a deeper shade

of pink, and she gnawed on her fist again. Landon was right about one thing. She definitely seemed hungry.

"It's okay, I'm here now." She dug through the supplies on the bed with one hand. Did her words mean anything to Adeline? Did her daughter even remember her? She pushed the hard questions away and spread a baby blanket on the bed to protect the quilt, then gently laid Adeline in the center.

She tried humming a lullaby, but Adeline was having none of it. Twisting onto her side, she wailed louder.

"It's okay, sweet girl." Kelsey kept one hand on Adeline as she stretched to reach the wipes and the diaper on the corner of the bed. Adeline rolled over onto her stomach and pushed up on her hands. Her crying echoed throughout the bedroom. Panic scratched and clawed its way through Kelsey's insides. Why couldn't she do this? She could dive to the depths of the ocean, repair a damaged submarine and recover artifacts from a shipwreck, but she couldn't change her own baby's diaper?

Hot tears stung her eyes.

"Please, Adeline," she whispered. "Let me do this one thing for you."

She gently redirected her baby onto her back. Adeline twisted out of her grasp again. Her pulse sped as another wave of frustration crested. Landon's steps moved closer. She quickly swiped at the moisture on her cheeks. She would *not* let him see her cry.

Landon strode back into the bedroom. "Here's the bottle of—"

Uh-oh. Kelsey sniffed and angled her head away. Was she crying?

"What's wrong?" He raised his voice to override Adeline's wailing.

"Nothing."

Adeline grabbed her toes with her fingers, blocking Kelsey's efforts. "Everything's fine. I'm just trying to put this stupid diaper on."

Adeline's screams escalated to a whole new pitch. Man, she sounded angry. Or hurt. His adrenaline spiked. Was she supposed to sound like that?

Landon set the warm bottle on the floor then stepped closer. He'd officially decided he couldn't handle his baby girl crying. It made him feel so helpless. Between Adeline's tears and the telltale moisture dotting Kelsey's skin, this whole situation had morphed from bad to worse.

"Do you want me to change her and you can give her the bottle?"

"No."

Landon bit back a frustrated groan. The woman had a stubborn streak a mile long. Maybe that's where Adeline got it. Probably best if he kept that thought to himself.

"Do you want me to help you?"

"No. Yes. I don't know." Kelsey's brow furrowed. "Was her skin this red the last time you changed her?"

Landon pushed his fingers through his hair. He had no idea. This wasn't the best time to admit he hadn't changed her lately. Hadn't the women in the church nursery taken care of that? He'd brought Adeline back from Wyoming and kept her alive for the past twenty-four hours. Didn't that count for anything?

"I think she has a diaper rash."

Landon's scalp prickled. *Great.* What did that mean?

Kelsey's eyes flashed. "We have to do something."

Wonderful. Another problem to solve. Kelsey'd probably find a way to blame him for this one, too.

"Does she have a diaper bag? Maybe there's some lotion or cream we can put on her skin."

Landon gestured to the baby supplies strewn across the room. "Everything you see here is what your mom sent. Her diaper bag's that gray backpack on the floor by the closet."

"Did you introduce any new foods?" Kelsey braced Adeline with one hand then leaned over and snagged the backpack with the other. "She isn't eating solids yet, right?"

"Actually, she's supposed to be eating that baby food stuff. Mixed with oatmeal or cereal or something."

Kelsey shot him a doubtful look. "Really?"

"I can show you your mom's instructions."

"It's fine. I believe you."

No, you don't.

Instead of arguing, Landon reached into the side pocket of the backpack, plucked out a pacifier and offered it to Adeline. She stopped crying and suckled away, the pink-and-white-dotted button bobbing up and down in her perfect little mouth. Well, look at that. At least he did one thing right.

Kelsey stared in disbelief, then twisted the cap off a small tube and applied a white paste to Adeline's splotchy red skin. Landon held his breath, bracing for more crying.

Adeline's face scrunched up and she fussed a little, then went back to sucking on her pacifier.

"There." Kelsey slid the tube back in the bag, cleaned her fingers with a wipe then quickly slid a new diaper into place. Landon stared. Amazing. How'd she do that so fast?

He sagged with relief. "I'd be glad to run to the store and get anything you feel Adeline needs."

"Perfect." Kelsey flashed the tiniest hint of a smile while she fastened the snaps on Adeline's outfit. "Diapers, wipes, formula, more of that diaper rash cream—"

"Hold on, hold on." Landon found some paper and a pencil in the drawer of his grandmother's old sewing table under the window and scrawled a list.

"I'm going to be gone about an hour or so." He picked up the bottle and handed it to Kelsey. "I need to know you'll be here when I get back."

She took her dear sweet time answering him, after huffing out an exasperated sigh. "I won't leave with Adeline, if that's what you're implying."

"Promise?"

She snatched the bottle from his hand. "You have my word."

"Good." He pocketed the list then followed her into the living room. She settled on the sofa with Adeline, who was already drinking from the bottle like she hadn't eaten in days. Kelsey ignored him while he lingered behind the sofa, her attention riveted on the baby nestled in the crook of her arm. *Their* baby. His chest pinched. They'd created a child together.

"I've got this." Her voice sounded raw. She cleared her throat. "You can go."

Her words chafed. "Not so fast."

She tipped her chin up, and he caught a glimpse of the emotion simmering below the surface of her hardened expression. He mentally swatted away the impatient words hovering like a wasp, waiting to sting.

Kelsey hadn't held her baby or fed her for months. She'd lost Wade and Maggie. Then he'd announced her stepfather had health issues and she'd grudgingly revealed Adeline belonged to him. That seemed like a lot for one person to process, even a woman as strong and self-sufficient as Kelsey.

Go easy on her, a subtle voice prompted.

He'd learned to heed that wise voice in recent months.

"I'd like for you and Adeline to stay here tonight."

"Not happening."

"Don't worry, I'll bunk at my parents' place. You and Adeline can have the guest room."

She glanced at the clock on the mantel. "I was really hoping to get on the road after supper."

No. Way. He wanted to stomp his foot like his friend Gage's son, Connor, did when he didn't get his way. Instead, he calmly ran his fingertips along his jaw. "How many hours have you been traveling? You must be exhausted. Should you really be driving in a storm at night with a baby?"

Irritation flickered in her eyes.

"I'm sure you're anxious to see your folks and all." He stopped short of mentioning her stepfather's stroke. "Get some rest and we'll map out a plan tomorrow."

Kelsey stared him down. His mind raced, already scrambling for a backup strategy to convince her to stay in case she refused.

"All right." She relented. "Just for tonight."

"I'll be back as soon as I can." He sidestepped another confrontation and grabbed his keys on the way out the door.

Outside, rain spattered his face as he jogged toward

his truck parked beside Kelsey's rental car. Doubt tormented him. Letting Kelsey and Adeline spend some time together was the right thing to do. Wasn't it?

He climbed into the truck's cab then started the engine. Hesitating, he glanced at the house one more time. She'd stay, wouldn't she?

Guilt mixed with the doubt, drawing another frustrated groan as he shifted the truck into gear. He had no business questioning Kelsey's trustworthiness, given the way he'd misled, fibbed and failed to show up too many times while he'd been addicted to pills. Yet she'd kept Adeline a secret.

Adeline. He was someone's dad. This news shifted his whole world. Now he had an even stronger motivation to stay clean and sober.

He wasn't going to lose his daughter.

Chapter Three

Kelsey blinked against the bright light streaming into the unfamiliar bedroom. As the picture on the opposite wall came into focus, reality parted the dense fog of her deep sleep.

Adeline.

Kelsey fumbled for her phone buried under the covers. Nine fifteen. How had she slept for almost eleven hours? And why didn't she hear Adeline cry? Did she sleep through the night? Was she still breathing?

The questions flooded her mind as she sat up, flung the covers aside and stumbled to the portable crib. It was empty. Panic squeezed her chest. Where was her baby?

Landon had taken her. He sneaked in during the night, scooped Adeline up and—

Stop. Calm down. Just breathe. She coached herself out of a full-on freak-out while she yanked a sweatshirt from her suitcase then slipped it on over her pajamas. Her feet slapped against the hardwood as she hurried down the hallway. Pausing in the kitchen, she quickly scanned the groceries that Landon had brought last night still stacked on the counter. The high chair in the corner beside the oval table sat empty. She surveyed the rest of the kitchen, hoping to see a dirty dish or an empty bottle. Some evidence that Landon had been here. Nope. Nothing. A throbbing ache in her forehead reminded her she'd gone far too long without any caffeine. That would have to wait. She had to find her daughter.

Where had Landon taken her?

They should've exchanged phone numbers last night. She'd been too exhausted to think clearly. He'd left after he dropped off the groceries. She shouldn't have trusted him. Now he was probably long gone.

She quickly trounced the negative thoughts. There had to be a more plausible explanation. If he'd left town with Adeline, why leave all the baby food, diapers and formula behind? She didn't remember meeting Landon's parents at Wade and Maggie's wedding, but that wouldn't stop her from marching over to their house and asking about their son and granddaughter.

They knew about Adeline, didn't they?

She found her flip-flops by the front door and slipped them on. Landon said they lived close. She assumed that meant walking distance. Hopefully it wasn't far. She wasn't thrilled about meeting them in her pajamas, but she couldn't waste time changing clothes.

She yanked open the front door, and a wall of hot air enveloped her.

"Good morning."

Landon's deep voice startled her, and she yelped. She turned slowly, following the subtle creaking sound. He sat on the wooden swing at the far end of the porch, rocking with Adeline snuggled in his arms.

Relief washed over her.

"Hey." She found her voice and padded toward them, noting the empty bottle on the porch beside the swing. Adeline slept, her pink mouth wide-open and chubby arms nested across her chest. The picture of contentment. Kelsey tried not to let her gaze linger on Landon's tanned forearms or the red T-shirt hugging his muscular shoulders. She shouldn't have allowed her eyes to wander to the appealing planes of his clean-shaven face either.

Her pulse sped as his hazel eyes met hers. The tip of his mouth curved up in a half smile—almost as if he'd caught her staring.

"Sleep well?"

She nodded, crossing her arms over the navy logo on her sweatshirt. "Except I was so worried when I woke up and she wasn't in the crib."

His smile faded. "I came by at five thirty, and she was starting to fuss. I thought I'd let you sleep. I'm sorry if I worried you."

His kindness sent a feeling of warmth zipping through her. Now she really regretted wearing the bulky sweatshirt. She had no idea Colorado was this hot in the summer.

"My mom brought you some breakfast." Landon held up something wrapped in aluminum foil. "Do you like breakfast burritos?"

"I'll eat anything," she said, resisting the urge to snatch the food from his hands.

"There's a travel mug with coffee under the swing." He passed her the burrito. "If you like cream and sugar, I have both inside."

"Thank you." She took the food. Why was he being

so nice? "My head is about to explode from lack of caffeine."

"Well, we can't have that." Landon tapped the porch with his boot to stop the swing's momentum. "Grab the coffee and have a seat."

She hesitated, then picked up the silver insulated mug and sank onto the wide wooden slats beside him.

Her heart expanded at the sight of her baby girl asleep in his arms. She couldn't stop staring at Adeline's flawless porcelain skin or the rosy-pink color on her smooth cheeks. Even her yellow-and-white-striped pajamas were adorable.

Landon chuckled and shifted Adeline in his arms like he held a fragile bouquet of delicate flowers. "She's perfect, right?"

"Sure is." Her words fell woefully short of describing the love she felt for her daughter. *Their* daughter. But thinking for long about the child they'd created together sent her tiptoeing into dangerous territory. Enemy territory.

She unwrapped the burrito and took a generous bite. Mainly because she was famished and eating kept her from speaking and aligning with Landon any more than she already had.

They rocked in silence while she savored the explosion of flavors in her burrito. The scrambled eggs, cheese and a hint of spicy sausage tasted incredible. When was the last time someone had brought her breakfast? She couldn't recall. As she reached for the coffee and took a sip, she sneaked another glance at Landon. While she couldn't figure out his intentions, she had to admit he looked awfully good holding a baby. It definitely upped his appeal.

Quit. This is the kind of thinking that only gets you in trouble. Remember?

She averted her gaze, then savored a long sip of coffee and took another bite of her burrito. Across the dirt road, fields of wheat stretched in every direction, dancing in the breeze. Huge wind turbines dotted the land. Their silver blades caught the sunlight and glinted as they spun.

Despite the shade of the porch, a rivulet of sweat trickled down her spine.

"I can hold Adeline for a few more minutes, then I need to get to work," Landon said.

"Where do you work?"

"Here." He tipped his head toward the fields she'd just admired. "My family is prepping to harvest all that wheat."

"When?"

"Probably in the next week or so."

"What are you going to do with Adeline?" Surely babies weren't supposed to ride in combines or tractors.

"I meant what I said last night. You and Adeline can stay here. We—"

"No way." Kelsey shot him her best you-have-got-to-be-kidding-me look. "We are not going to play house."

"You didn't let me finish." Landon kept his voice low but stopped the swing. "I'll stay with my parents and you can stay here with Adeline."

She really, *really* wanted to say no. Her burrito sat half-finished in her hand. Her appetite had fled. "We aren't a family, Landon. We barely know each other. Let's stop pretending."

"I'm not pretending anything." His voice grew strained. Adeline cried out, and they both stilled, paralyzed by the potential interruption in her nap. At least they agreed that her sleep took precedence.

The chains creaked as Landon set the swing in motion again.

"I want to go home," Kelsey whispered.

"You can go home, but you're not taking Adeline."

Anger surged. "You can't make that decision."

"Please, Kelsey." His expression softened. "I just found out I'm her dad. Stay until harvest is over. Then we can make a plan, one we can both live with."

"I don't want to stay in your house," she said. It felt too intimate. Too personal.

"My sister's house is close by. I'll ask her if you and Adeline can stay there for a little while."

"I don't want to stay with your sister, either."

"She doesn't live there. She's married and has twins. They live in a house her husband already owned. Never mind. Long story. Her house is modern and more convenient for having a baby around and still has a lot of her furniture in it."

"Sounds too good to be true." She tapped her fingertip on the top of the coffee mug. "What's the catch?"

Landon's brow furrowed. "No catch. You can have your own space and we can both see Adeline."

She sighed. "I don't know. This feels like a bizarre custody arrangement."

"That's because this is a bizarre situation."

"I really want to go home and see my mom and stepdad, especially if my stepdad isn't well."

"You can leave if you want. But Adeline stays with me."

You're out of your mind. The harsh words zipped through her head. Somehow, she kept them from slipping out of her mouth. That would only escalate into a heated argument. And she didn't want to fight. They couldn't keep circling each other like two stubborn mules, though. There had to be a compromise.

"I'm sorry about your stepdad's stroke. And I hate that Wade and Maggie are gone," Landon said. "Adeline's lost a lot, too. She needs stability. Why not give her what she needs? Here she'll have her mom and her dad, plus extended family to take care of her."

"She has family in Wyoming, too." Kelsey twisted to face him. "I'm not taking her from you. You can visit whenever you want."

"Which means never." Landon raked his fingers through his blond hair. "Your parents' ranch is six hours away. I can't drop by after work. Besides, you don't get to be the only one who decides what's best for our daughter."

Kelsey couldn't argue with that. Or the part about Adeline needing stability. Why did he have to be so reasonable? She'd mentally prepared for charming. She'd expected the not-a-care-in-the-world version of Landon. What was she supposed to do with this prudent, logical version?

"All right." She pushed out a long breath. "Adeline and I will stay at your sister's place, but only for two weeks. Then we're going home."

Two weeks.

He had exactly two weeks to convince Kelsey that he was worthy of fatherhood and Adeline belonged with him. Not impossible, right? He'd conquered tougher obstacles than her fierce determination. And she was clearly determined to take Adeline back to Wyoming.

Uneasiness slithered through him like a rattlesnake in a wheat field. She'd agreed to stay. That was almost too simple. He stole a sidelong glance. Kelsey looked stunning, even in her sweatshirt and gray gym shorts. Her dark hair tumbled in messy waves past her shoulders and her cheeks were flushed an appealing shade of pink.

Sitting together on the porch swing while she drank her coffee and he held their baby teased him with a sneak peek of the kind of future he'd dreamed about. This nearly perfect scenario almost fooled him. Almost convinced him that he had a shot at a happily-ever-after. With her.

"What changed your mind?"

"What do you mean?"

"When you got here last night, you couldn't wait to leave and take Adeline with you. What did I say to change your mind?"

Kelsey's eyes narrowed. "Don't give yourself too much credit, cowboy. I'm doing what's best for Adeline. And you won't convince me to stay longer, so don't even try."

Ha. Challenge accepted. He dragged a hand over his face to smother a smile. "I was a bull rider, but those days are over."

"Do you miss it?"

"Bull riding?" He lifted one shoulder, trying to dismiss her question. Her inquiry surprised him. And he didn't want to talk about it. Not now. Not with her. He looked away, trapped in the memory of his last ride. Yeah, he missed doing the thing he was made to do. How could he not?

The anticipation that hummed in his veins before

the gate swung open and the bull shot into the arena in a bone-rattling trajectory. The heady rush of adrenaline as he fought to stay on the enraged animal, then the thrill of victory when the whistle blasted and the crowd roared. Success had brought many blessings, which he'd squandered on foolish investments and a cunning addiction.

"It was a good ride," he said quietly. "But that's all in the past. Now I want to settle down and carry on the family tradition of farming this land."

There. He'd told her what he wanted. Now that he knew about Adeline, he'd refine his focus. Getting out of debt and providing for his daughter were his new priorities.

"We'll have to figure out how to coparent," she said.

Coparenting. Such a hollow word. He hated it already. Along with *custody*, *paternity test* and *child support*. All the unfamiliar terms he'd scrolled through on the internet when he'd stayed up way too late the night before, researching his options. Did he need to hire an attorney?

"The clock's ticking." Kelsey plowed on before he formulated an answer. "I have fifty-seven days to establish a new family care plan and submit it to my commanding officer."

"And if you don't?"

"If I don't what?"

"If you don't submit the care plan or whatever it's called. What will happen?"

"I'll be discharged without benefits."

"What?" Her words slammed into him. "That's crazy."

"It's the truth. Involuntary separation by reason of

parenthood." She sighed. "I won't let that happen. I need the health insurance, the housing, all the benefits. Plus, I want to take advantage of the GI Bill when I'm out of the navy so I can go to nursing school."

"You lose all that if you don't prove your child is well cared for?"

She nodded. "The military wants confirmation that I'll honor my service commitment and that my child is safe and thriving."

"How much longer are you enlisted for?"

"I can get out in October of next year."

He mentally calculated the time. Fifteen months? That was way too long to shuffle Adeline back and forth like a piece of cargo. Yet another reason why he wanted her to stay here with him.

His phone chimed from where he'd left it balanced on the porch railing. "That's probably my dad checking in. We need a part for the combine, and I promised him I'd run to town and pick it up."

"Oh."

Was she disappointed? Seemed like she'd be more than happy to have some time alone. Time without him around, anyway. He shot her another glance. Her gaze slid to Adeline, still asleep in his arms. "I'll hold her."

He stood and carefully transferred Adeline into Kelsey's waiting arms. He held his breath, willing her to stay asleep. When his fingers brushed against Kelsey's, he stepped back, eager to put some distance between them.

She stared down at Adeline, her mouth tipping up in a half smile. Landon pushed out a long breath and turned to leave.

"Landon?"

He hesitated. The sound of his name on her lips halted his steps.

"Thanks for breakfast."

"You're welcome." He didn't turn around. His boots clomped on the porch as he left the house and strode toward his truck.

The morning sun warmed his skin. He slid behind the wheel, turned the key in the ignition and cranked the air-conditioning. Kelsey had made her feelings and her plans as clear as the Colorado sky overhead. She seemed so strong. So confident and self-assured. He'd felt like that once. Invincible. The king of the world. Oh, how he'd crashed and burned. Evidently, she had her future all planned out, and it didn't include leaving their daughter in Merritt's Crossing.

"Spoiler alert, beautiful girl." His words echoed through the truck's cab as he drove away. "You can't control everything."

While he respected Kelsey's choice to serve their country and the terms of her military commitment were nonnegotiable, they shared a child. Nothing could sever that bond. And no matter what Kelsey believed, he'd prove he could take care of Adeline.

Doubt nagged him as he drove toward town. An eight-second ride on a ferocious beast seemed easier than convincing Kelsey that Adeline should stay with him.

Chapter Four

What had she done?

Rooted to Landon's porch swing, Kelsey drained the last of the coffee in the insulated mug. Two birds soared over the empty dirt road. She was feeling uncomfortably warm, but Adeline slept so peacefully in her arms, she didn't want to move. Landon had driven away a while ago, his truck tires kicking up a cloud of dust in his wake. The reality of their agreement tugged at her, like an anchor weighing her down.

In the navy, she'd helped recover submerged aircraft and inspected damaged hulls in the darkest depths of the ocean. Spending a couple of weeks in Merritt's Crossing couldn't be that difficult. Especially if Landon's family sweetened the deal with a house for her and Adeline. They needed their own space. Scratch that, she needed her own space. Landon's gorgeous eyes and that megawatt smile proved to be her kryptonite. *How* had he talked her into changing her plans?

Already exhausted from the mental tug-of-war raging inside her head, she sighed and pushed to her feet. Second-guessing her choices was unproductive, yet the uncertainty camped out in her gut made her legs itch with the urge to run all the way to her parents' place in Wyoming. Except Landon's words echoing in her head about giving Adeline stability grounded her, like a plane prohibited from flying.

As much as she hated to admit it, he was right. Besides, he'd had less than twenty-four hours to adjust to the news that he was Adeline's father. Staying close by and giving them both the opportunity to work out a co-parenting plan was the best option for her baby. Plus, she couldn't help but feel that Landon's kindness and pragmatic approach to meeting Adeline's needs had to be a cover-up. And Kelsey wouldn't rest until she exposed his ulterior motives.

She headed inside, leaving the mug and the remnants of her breakfast to come back and grab later. Cradling Adeline gently in the crook of her arm, she closed the heavy front door quietly. The hum of a window AC unit greeted her. An oscillating fan sat on the floor in the living room, twisting back and forth. Kelsey welcomed the air as it skimmed her face. Had Landon turned on the fan when he'd dropped by earlier? She didn't like the thought of him being in the house while she slept, but it was his house. And he'd graciously let her stay the night with Adeline and had taken care of their daughter before he even knew she was his, so obviously he wasn't a total monster.

Maybe she had to cut him a little slack. He hadn't gone ballistic, and he'd made sure she had coffee, breakfast and a place to live.

Stay vigilant. Don't let him worm his way into your good graces.

Adeline stirred in her arms, snapping Kelsey out of

her pep talk. She stared at her baby girl. Oh, her heart. She didn't know it had the capacity to expand with just one look at her daughter. Adeline's eyes fluttered open, and her brow furrowed as she focused on Kelsey's face. Landon and his grand gestures would have to be analyzed some other time. She'd been given precious moments alone with Adeline, and she didn't want to waste another minute worrying about Landon.

"Hey, sweet pea," Kelsey cooed. "Did you have a good nap?"

Adeline's expression crumpled, then her skin flushed pink and she started to cry.

Oh no. She hadn't expected the crying. When her family sent her pictures, Adeline almost always looked happy. Content. In all Kelsey's daydreams about her reunion with her daughter, somehow she'd only imagined bubbly baby giggles and heartwarming snuggles.

So far, their time together had been exactly the opposite. Instead, whenever Adeline saw Kelsey, she cried. More sweat dampened Kelsey's skin, and she tamped down the panic clawing at her insides.

Think. C'mon, think. She hummed a lullaby and swayed awkwardly side to side, already feeling ridiculous. Good thing Landon wasn't here, because he'd probably laugh. Adeline cried louder, her chubby fist clenching.

"Hang on, sweet girl. I'm out of practice." Kelsey strode down the hall toward the bedroom.

A pacifier sat abandoned in the corner of the portable crib. Kelsey snagged it then touched it to Adeline's mouth. She screamed and thrust her head to the side.

All righty then.

Kelsey grabbed the backpack from the floor, then

shoved the rumpled blankets aside and gently placed Adeline in the center of the bed. Landon might've come up with the perfect changing station in the corner, but there was no way she'd put Adeline up on the dresser.

Thankfully the bag had everything she needed. As soon as the package of wipes crinkled in Kelsey's hand, Adeline twisted out of her grasp. Pathetic tears slid from the corners of her eyes.

"Adeline, it's okay." Kelsey tried to stay calm, but the squirming and the crying tested her patience. Why was this so hard? Shouldn't a mother be able to change her baby's diaper without an epic meltdown?

A few agonizing minutes later, hot tears burned her eyelids, but she'd managed to treat Adeline's rash and get her into a clean diaper. Kelsey scooped her up, planted a kiss on her damp cheek, then carried her into the kitchen.

Adeline slurped on her thumb while Kelsey surveyed the groceries on the counter. Landon had mentioned notes from her mother. Where did he leave those? The jars of baby food, rice cereal and cans of formula overwhelmed her. She might be Adeline's mother, but she had no idea how to feed a baby anything other than a bottle.

The options were limited. Call Landon or call her mother. Adeline bounced up and down in Kelsey's arms and fussed.

"Are you hungry?" Kelsey turned in a circle, trying to remember where she'd left her phone.

While getting home to Adeline had consumed her thoughts since she'd left the base, the news about her stepfather had struck her like a curveball she never saw coming. Her mother's decision to keep his challenges a secret shredded her. Which was ironic, considering the secret she'd carried for eighteen months. But her reasons made sense. Landon had basically left her with a lame excuse scratched on a notepad, and her own stepbrother had supplied plenty of wild stories about Landon's addiction-fueled antics.

Her mother didn't need to hide her stepfather's health problems. Kelsey was a strong, independent woman, capable of carrying heavy burdens. Why hadn't they told her? And when was the memorial service for Wade and Maggie? She'd hoped to put off calling until she wasn't so wound up. Or still reeling from their lie of omission.

But Adeline wasn't going to put up with her indecisiveness much longer. And Kelsey wasn't willing to risk making any more mistakes. She heaved a sigh and trudged back to her bedroom, plucked her phone from the nightstand and scrolled to her mother's number. She might be upset with her mother's choices, and she really hated asking for help, but she would set her feelings aside if it meant finding out how to feed her baby properly.

Landon eased his truck into a parking spot near Tomlinson's Furniture in downtown Merritt's Crossing and turned off the ignition. He'd picked up the part for the combine at the store like his father had asked him to, and he needed to grab lunch and get back to the farm soon. But first he needed to stop in the furniture store and buy a crib for Adeline.

"I'm buying a crib," he whispered, shaking his head in disbelief. "For my daughter." He still hadn't quite wrapped his brain around all the ways Kelsey's arrival and her confession had turned his world upside down.

His sister Laramie's best friend Skye owned her family's furniture store. Her husband, Gage, helped out some, too. They probably had a new crib in stock. And if they were sold out, maybe they knew of one he'd be able to borrow. Between their family plus Jack and Laramie's twins, there had to be at least one extra crib somewhere. Adeline didn't seem to mind the portable crib he'd brought with her from the ranch, but he wanted her to have something more permanent.

He gripped the door handle and hesitated before getting out of the truck. As soon as he asked Skye and Gage about a crib, they'd want to know why. Nothing stayed a secret in Merritt's Crossing for long, but he wasn't sure he was ready to spread the news that the baby in his house belonged to him.

Adeline's mother showing up unexpectedly on his doorstep, reminding him of the sins of his past, only added more fuel to the fire of guilt raging inside. Gage and Skye were no strangers to the notion of caring for a baby who needed a home. That was exactly how Connor had become a part of their family. They wouldn't judge him. And Landon had at least a dozen questions to ask them about the legal issues surrounding Adeline's arrival, Kelsey's commitment to the military and his rights as the biological father. Not that Gage and Skye handed out legal advice with their furniture sales. Gage had served in the navy, and Connor's adoption had included some complicated layers, based on what Landon had heard from Laramie. Despite his convoluted feelings, he'd come to the right place.

"Lord, I need help. Again." Pausing to pray before he barreled ahead had saved him some heartache over the last several months. His addiction had infused him with a false sense of confidence. He'd said and done so many things he regretted while he was high on pills. He squeezed his eyes shut to block the familiar wave of shame. While undoing his past mistakes wasn't an option, he wanted to make wise choices for his future. Especially with Adeline. And Kelsey, too. He hated that his careless behavior had made her feel like she had no other option than to keep their daughter a secret from him.

"Enough with the stalling, Chambers," he grumbled under his breath. He'd made so many mistakes and fallen so far off his pedestal that he should be well past worrying what people thought or said about him. Besides, he'd taken Adeline to church and let her stay in the nursery yesterday, so that probably launched the gossip train out of the station. He could handle the curious stares. Even a little whispering behind hands didn't bother him.

But Kelsey wasn't from here. She hadn't signed up for that kind of scrutiny. Despite his anger and confusion over her keeping Adeline a secret, he cared about her. If she was going to be in town even for a little while, he felt compelled to protect her. To shield her.

Cars and trucks cruised by on Main Street as he strode down the sidewalk toward the furniture store. Red, white and blue bunting draped the storefronts while the American flags mounted on the streetlight poles snapped in the warm breeze. The Fourth of July celebrations had ended, but the decorations remained, a tribute to Merritt's Crossing's patriotism.

Landon waved to a friend of his dad's headed into the pharmacy. Most folks he'd passed wore the same focused expressions. With a long stretch of warm weather in the forecast, farmers and their families, along with the hired help, were gearing up for harvesting wheat.

He quickened his steps. All the more reason to buy a crib for Adeline then get back to the farm with that part for the combine. Dad had a lengthy to-do list to knock out, and Landon had promised he'd help.

Bells jingled as he opened the door to the furniture store and stepped inside. A floral scent enveloped him, probably from the giant candle flickering on the table nearby.

"I'll be with you in a minute." Skye's muffled voice filtered toward him from the office.

"No problem," he called out then worked his way across the showroom to the section where Skye had arranged a nursery and a kid's bedroom.

The bunk beds stacked against the wall with matching blue and red plaid comforters, coupled with the red wire bin filled with a stuffed basketball, soccer ball and football, and pendants on the wall featuring some of Colorado's favorite sports teams made Landon smile. Skye sure knew how to stage a kid's room. A denim beanbag, a rainbow-colored stack of wooden blocks and a few books filled the corner next to the beds.

Landon turned in a slow circle. The nursery furniture nearly took him to his knees. The crib, dresser and rocking chair were all painted white. He'd never seen so much pink and gray stuff in one room. The sheets in the crib, the stuffed animals on the chair, even the letters mounted on the wall above the changing table all had the same pink and gray pattern.

And elephants. He'd never associated elephants with nursery decor, but Skye made it all look perfect. If this was the standard for Adeline's room, he had a lot of work to do. Not to mention money to invest.

His stomach twisted at the thought. He already had a significant debt to pay off. Now he'd need to focus on saving for Adeline, too.

"Landon?"

He turned at the sound of Skye's voice.

She smiled and strode toward him. "I thought that was you. What brings you by?"

"I need a crib." Landon palmed the back of his neck. "Today, if possible."

Surprise flashed in her blue eyes. "Really."

"Laramie didn't tell you?"

Skye shook her head. "Gage and I were out of town for a few days, so I haven't talked to her since we got home. What's up?"

Landon pushed out a long breath. "Long story short, I became the guardian for my friend Wade's baby girl when he and his wife passed away unexpectedly."

Skye gasped.

"Oh, wait." He held up his hand. "It gets even more exciting. Last night, a woman I'd met at Wade's wedding showed up at the house claiming the baby was hers. And mine." Warmth heated his skin. Skye had been his sister's best friend for as long as he could remember. His mistakes and shortcomings were no secret. Still, admitting that his reckless decisions had impacted other people stung. No matter how many times the truth smacked him in the face.

Skye's expression filled with empathy. "That's a lot to process all at once, isn't it?"

"Yeah." He resisted the temptation to blast her with a truckload of questions. She and Gage had shared caregiving responsibilities for Connor, the little boy they eventually adopted. From what he'd heard, that process hadn't been all rainbows and unicorns. Yet they'd worked it out and ended up falling in love and getting married.

Not that he wanted to marry Kelsey. At all. She'd never trust him, much less settle down here. They had completely different goals. But they did need to figure out how to care for Adeline without choking each other.

"You look like you've got a lot on your mind," Skye said. "Want me to pick out a crib and have Gage deliver it?"

He wanted to hug her. "That would be awesome."

"I'm not sure I have anything in stock." She walked toward the front of the store. "Let me check. We can add rush delivery, but it still might take seven to ten days."

"Seven to ten *days*?" He trailed after her, his voice lifting in shock.

"Sorry." She glanced over her shoulder and scrunched her nose. "That's probably not what you wanted to hear."

Landon propped his hip against a sectional sofa displayed in the middle of the showroom and weighed his options. He didn't have a strong opinion where Adeline slept. As long as she slept. And wasn't in any danger. Since Kelsey had balked at his modified changing station, he figured she'd want Adeline to have a crib. Going back to the house without making arrangements for one seemed like yet another reason for him and Kelsey to argue. And he'd like to avoid more confrontation if possible.

Skye's manicured nails clacked over her laptop's keys. "What's your daughter's name?"

"Adeline."

"Beautiful." She glanced up at him. "Where's she sleeping now?"

"In one of those portable things. I brought it from her grandmother's house. That's the only thing that would fit in my truck along with all the other baby stuff."

Skye laughed. "Babies require a lot of stuff."

"You're telling me."

"So you'd like to have this delivered to the farm-house?"

"Actually, no. It needs to go to Laramie's place. Adeline's going to stay there with her mother."

Skye's eyes widened. "Does Laramie know?"

He nodded. "She gave me permission."

"I wasn't implying that you needed permission." Skye reached for her phone. "Let me double-check, but I'm almost positive there's already a crib in one of the bedrooms. She ended up with two, but the twins shared one, and she needed someplace to store the extra. I'll text her real quick."

While Skye pecked out a message, Landon mentally pieced together the puzzle. His nieces, Macey and Charlotte, were three now and had graduated to big-girl beds. He'd heard all about it the last time he visited. If there was something available for Adeline to sleep in, then he didn't need to worry about buying a crib. Unless he and Kelsey planned to iron out a temporary custody agreement where Adeline spent a few nights a week with him.

Drat. Another scenario where he and Kelsey probably wouldn't see eye to eye. But he was Adeline's father. He needed to be available. He *wanted* to be available. And it wasn't fair to expect Kelsey to handle a majority of the parenting, even though that was probably her preference.

He was no longer a competitive bull rider or the impulsive, irresponsible groomsman Kelsey had met at Wade's wedding. He'd prove he had changed. He'd prove to Kelsey—and himself—that he could be a reliable, trustworthy dad.

Gravel crunched under tires and engines rumbled outside, pulling Kelsey toward the living room window in Landon's farmhouse. Adeline squealed and maneuvered across the floor on her belly, an adorable little inchworm with elbows. Kelsey chuckled and stopped to admire her baby girl. Again. Since her phone call to her mother went straight to voice mail, Kelsey had fumbled her way through feeding Adeline baby food for the first time. It wasn't as terrifying as she'd thought.

Then they'd spent the last hour camped out in the middle of the living room floor, examining every single thing Adeline managed to reach or grab. Mostly, Kelsey loved draping one of her T-shirts on Adeline's head then gently tugging it off and savoring the delicious sound of Adeline's belly laugh. It was an entertaining game, one that kept Adeline from crying, so Kelsey would keep playing until they were both worn out. Anything to keep her little one content.

"C'mon, cutie patootie. Let's see who's here." Kelsey picked up Adeline, went to the front door and opened it. A petite blond-haired woman with a noticeable baby bump stood on the porch. Her bright green eyes immediately zoomed in on Adeline, then her chin wobbled, and she pressed her fingertips to her lips.

Oh boy. Kelsey shifted from one foot to the other.

Who was this pregnant, teary-eyed woman showing up at Landon's house unannounced?

"Hi, I'm Kelsey. Are you looking for Landon?"

The woman shook her head and sniffed, then braced her palms on her rounded abdomen. "I'm Laramie Tomlinson, Landon's sister. We probably met at Wade and Maggie's wedding."

Ah. She sagged with relief. For a second, she'd wondered if he had a pregnant girlfriend he'd conveniently omitted from last night's conversation.

Kelsey quickly scrolled through her mental snapshots from the wedding weekend. She didn't recall meeting Laramie. Of course, she'd pretty much been obsessed with Landon the entire time. Even though she'd never admit that now.

"So that makes you Adeline's aunt. I'm her mother, by the way." She shook Laramie's hand, but the woman couldn't take her eyes off Adeline. She immediately stole the spotlight by blowing raspberries with her adorable little mouth.

Laramie smiled and knuckled away a tear. "I'm sorry. You must think I'm ridiculous, crying at the sight of your baby. Pregnancy hormones are no joke."

"You're not wrong," Kelsey said. "I still remember what that was like. When are you due?"

"November twenty-fifth."

"Is this your first?"

"My husband, Jack, and I have twin girls who are three."

Another truck had pulled up and parked beside Laramie's vehicle. A man exited the driver's side, then slammed the door and strode toward them. Kelsey studied him, trying to assess his connection to Laramie and Landon.

"If you're looking for Landon, I'm not sure when he'll be back. He left after breakfast and said something about needing to buy parts for a combine."

"Hey, Drew." Laramie ignored Kelsey's comment and waved to the man. "This is my brother-in-law Drew Tomlinson. Drew, this is Kelsey and Adeline."

Kelsey offered him a polite smile as he joined Laramie on the porch. "What can I help you with?"

While she understood Landon's family and friends probably wanted to see Adeline, Kelsey would rather they didn't stick around. After their marathon play session, she desperately needed Adeline to take a solid afternoon nap. Kelsey's hand traveled to her hair, still piled in a messy bun. Then she glanced down and realized she had baby food spattered on her T-shirt and she was wearing the same shorts she'd slept in. A shower sounded amazing right now.

"It's nice to meet you," Drew said. "And this must be the baby girl I've heard so much about today." He reached out and skimmed his fingers across Adeline's arm.

Kelsey resisted the urge to step back. They'd had such a fun morning together. Selfishly, she didn't want Adeline to start crying again because strangers frightened her.

Adeline's perfect brow furrowed as her head swiveled between her arm and Drew's face.

Oh no. Kelsey held her breath. *Please don't cry.*

Laramie chuckled. "You're an observant little thing, aren't you?"

Adeline rewarded her with a toothy grin, then shoved

her thumb in her mouth and rested her head against Kelsey's shoulder. "I don't mean to be rude, but I need to get her down for her nap soon. Landon has his phone if you need to text him. Or I'm sure he'll be back later."

Laramie and Drew exchanged glances. "He's actually the one who asked us to come by. He said you might need some help getting settled at my place. Well, my old place." Laramie shrugged. "I'm glad you and Adeline are going to stay there. No reason for a cute house to sit empty."

"Wait." Kelsey shifted Adeline to her other hip. "Landon sent you to help me?"

"Sure did." Drew grinned. "My sister, Skye, heard you and Adeline might need a few things, too."

"We wanted to make sure you knew there was a crib at the house already. You're welcome to use anything that's there," Laramie said.

"News spreads like wildfire around here," Drew added. "I can almost guarantee the casserole committee is circling their wagons."

Kelsey's gaze pinged from Drew to Laramie. "A casserole committee?"

"He means meals," Laramie said. "Friends from church, neighbors, people who know our family will want to welcome you to Merritt's Crossing. You'll probably have a few ladies show up at your door this week with food."

"For what?"

"For you." Drew patted his flat stomach with his palm. "If I were you, I'd pray for Mrs. Wilkerson's peach cobbler and Mrs. Johnson's chicken salad."

"Oh." Kelsey could barely force out the single syllable. She tried to muster up an enthusiastic response, but the idea of more strangers bringing her meals and staring at her baby made her want to climb the walls. This might be Landon's hometown and his family might welcome outsiders, but that didn't mean she wanted to build connections or make new friends. Because sooner or later, Landon would fall back on his old habits, forcing her to leave to keep Adeline safe.

Chapter Five

"A friend from church just dropped these off." Landon set the box of diapers on the floor in Laramie's living room then straightened. Every muscle in his body ached. Between the early-morning visit with Adeline, working all afternoon on the farm and helping Kelsey move into Laramie's place, he'd pushed himself to the limit. He'd moved past hungry and onto famished, and a thin layer of dust coated his skin. Worse, his chronic back injury screamed at him to get off his feet.

But he wouldn't leave until he knew Kelsey felt settled. Comfortable. And the pinched expression on her face hinted that she wasn't happy.

"What's wrong?" He swiped at the sweat on his forehead with the sleeve of his T-shirt while Kelsey paced the living room, a cranky Adeline wedged on her hip.

"Nothing."

The telltale furrow in her brow betrayed her. There was most definitely something going on.

"Want me to hold her while you eat?"

Enough food to sustain a large family for a week

had paraded through the front door in the last couple of hours. Including Mrs. Wilkerson's peach cobbler.

His stomach growled.

Kelsey shot him a knowing look. "I'm not hungry, but if you are, help yourself."

Landon hesitated. Did she mean that? Everything about her vibe screamed, *leave me alone!* But he was starving. Besides, he felt bad about leaving when Adeline seemed fussy.

He glanced at the swing Drew had arranged in the corner near the window. With a miniature stuffed hippopotamus, giraffe and elephant dangling from the arm overhead, and a padded light green seat decorated with more safari-themed creatures, he couldn't imagine why Adeline wouldn't enjoy it. Laramie had mentioned the multiple speeds and its ability to play a cute lullaby and raved about how Charlotte and Macey had both loved the thing when they were little.

"Do you want to try putting her in the swing?" Landon asked. "It might help with the crying."

Kelsey cast a suspicious glance toward the contraption, as if sizing up whether it was qualified to hold her precious baby girl.

Landon held in a groan. After all they had done for her—helping her move and get settled, providing food and every possible piece of equipment they could think of for Adeline—a little gratitude might be nice.

Don't pick a fight, man. Just don't, he mentally coached himself as he crossed the room to the swing and fiddled with the settings. He wasn't going to provoke Kelsey, no matter how tempted he was to confront her about her sour attitude.

A few seconds later, a familiar soothing tune played

from the small speaker. Adeline swiveled in Kelsey's arms, gnawing on one of her fingers while she stared at the swing. Her fussing had stopped.

Relief flooded through him, and he couldn't stop himself from flashing Kelsey a victorious smile. "See? She's a fan already."

"Or maybe she just likes the music."

Oh brother. Landon felt his smile slide from his face like an ice cream cone melting on a hot summer day. Did she have to crush every one of his suggestions? He turned away and scanned the swing. Was it not safe? Straps with plastic buckles protruded from the seat. Those looked like they'd pass a thorough inspection. There were no sharp objects within a fifty-foot radius. He'd even arranged the blinds to keep the late-afternoon sun from blasting Adeline in the face.

Although to be honest, the land of baby equipment was so foreign, he really didn't know what to look for. As a former professional bull rider who'd lived for the adrenaline rush of riding a savage beast, safety had admittedly never been his top priority.

Until now. Until he had become a father.

"You can trust my sister," he said quietly. "She wouldn't loan you anything that wasn't safe."

Kelsey quirked her lips to one side. "All right, I suppose we can try it. Just for a few minutes, though."

She skirted the coffee table as she crossed the room, then carefully lowered Adeline into the seat.

Adeline kicked her bare legs and cooed at the animals dangling over her head while Kelsey buckled her in.

"I'm sure this will be fine." Kelsey straightened but kept hovering, as if Adeline needed her to stand by and avert the next impending disaster.

"Then why are you so irritated? Did you have a bad experience with baby swings?"

He instantly regretted his lame attempt at making a joke when Kelsey turned and walked toward the kitchen, her bare feet smacking out a determined rhythm on the hardwood floor.

He followed her. "You're not superhuman, Kels. She'll be okay if she uses a baby swing, especially if you need to eat or spend a few minutes by yourself."

"I've been away from her for months, remember?"

She snatched a pie-shaped container wrapped in aluminum foil and plastic wrap from the counter then slid it into the freezer without looking at him. "That's plenty of time by myself. Plenty of time to feel guilty and worry about whether I'm making the right decisions."

"Ah, now we're getting somewhere." He propped his shoulder against the door frame, grimacing as pain zinged from his lower back down his leg, hot and fierce. Her feistiness was a little easier to overlook once he realized she'd lashed out because of her fear and uncertainty. He wasn't a big fan of fear, either. Trying to ride an angry bull had never *not* terrified him. And being a parent proved equally frightening.

That didn't mean he'd give up, though. And he wasn't about to let Kelsey keep hiding behind her protective walls—no matter how hard she fought to maintain her emotional distance. Deep down, he knew he could be the father their daughter needed. Maybe even the kind of man Kelsey needed.

She ignored him and scooped up three plastic containers of what appeared to be brownies and cookies and shoved them in the pantry. Next, she opened every single cabinet in Laramie's kitchen. They were all empty.

Laramie had left quite a bit of furniture, but she'd taken all her personal belongings, including almost everything in the kitchen, with her when she'd moved out.

Landon still kept his distance, silently hoping no casseroles or desserts were harmed while she vented her frustration on the donations spread across the granite countertop.

Kelsey pulled back the aluminum foil on a pan of macaroni and cheese sitting on top of the stove. A tendril of steam curled into the air.

"Do you want some?" she asked, brandishing a paper plate she'd discovered in a stack on the counter.

"I'll get it. You don't have to serve me." He moved closer, but Adeline released an earsplitting wail, halting his steps.

Kelsey looked up at him. The pain swimming in her eyes caught him off guard. "She doesn't need that swing. She needs us."

Whoa. Adeline's crying really bothered her. This glimpse of Kelsey's tender concern for their daughter sent him back to the living room. "You eat. I'll get her."

While every stride ratcheted up the pain gripping his lower back, Landon couldn't possibly leave now. Because if he left while Adeline was screaming, then he'd prove Kelsey right. He'd show he was selfish and unreliable. Besides, her words pierced him like an arrow of truth.

She needs us.

He and Kelsey might not agree on much, but he couldn't argue with that. Adeline needed her mother and her father. There was no way he'd miss out on an opportunity to comfort their sweet baby girl. Or give Kelsey any more reasons to discredit him.

* * *

Why? *Why* was he still here?

Annoyance flared, burning through her veins. Hadn't he played the hero enough today?

Suddenly famished, Kelsey rummaged in a container of kitchen supplies Landon's mother had dropped off earlier and found a serving spoon. Then she loaded a generous serving of macaroni and cheese onto her plate and added salad plus a dollop of dressing from the container someone had brought along with the macaroni and cheese.

When she turned from the stove, her plate nearly slid from her hands. Landon's pale blue T-shirt stretched across his broad shoulders as he leaned over and scooped Adeline from the swing.

"Hey, pretty girl." His voice was low and soft, those strong, capable hands suddenly gentle as he cocooned Adeline against his shoulder and pressed a kiss to the top of her head.

Kelsey's traitorous insides puddled.

"I'll take her outside so you can eat." Landon crossed the living room in long strides, then opened the sliding glass door and stepped out onto the deck.

"Thank you." She managed to force out the words, but Landon had already closed the door. He patted Adeline's back while he walked slowly across the wooden deck burnished to a coppery brown from the hot sunshine. The skirt of Adeline's yellow sleeveless dress fluttered in the breeze. As he changed directions, Kelsey caught a glimpse of his lips moving. Was he singing? No matter how much his presence aggravated her, Kelsey couldn't look away.

The heat from her food warmed her hand through

the thin paper plate, and she slid it back onto the counter. She picked out a plastic fork from a bag of utensils lying beside the disposable cups and plates contributed by yet another stranger and dug in. While she'd claimed she wasn't hungry, her body proved otherwise. She devoured the meal standing up as though she hadn't eaten in days. The crispy bread-crumb crust topping the creamy macaroni and cheese was amazing and reminded her of her mom's cooking. Kelsey paused midbite, closed her eyes and released a satisfied sigh.

This was so not fair. Landon must've rallied his friends and family to woo her. *Well, nice try.* She wouldn't let them. Opening her eyes, she stabbed a bite of salad with her fork. Sure, Laramie's house was cute and conveniently located, and the amount of food that had arrived would feed a hungry platoon for days. The ladies who'd come with Landon's mom had even made up the bed in the guest room for her, and she couldn't believe how quickly they'd found sheets for the crib and a bin full of baby toys.

Their generosity wouldn't last, though. These ladies had only shown up for her because they didn't want Landon to lose Adeline. She hated that she'd grown so cynical. So jaded. But watching her father manipulate her mother for years, only to leave them hungry and alone while he disappeared for days or weeks, had taught her she couldn't afford to trust anyone.

She stole a glance through the sliding glass door. Landon stood facing Laramie's fenced backyard. Adeline had fallen asleep on his shoulder.

Kelsey's heart pinched. Why did he have to look so *good* holding her? Few things made her swoon—

but evidently an incredibly attractive man holding her baby girl was one.

Stop. Almost anyone could hold a sleeping infant for a few minutes. That didn't mean he could be a decent, reliable father for the long haul. She forced herself to look away, letting her gaze wander around the room. If she and Adeline had to stick around for a couple of weeks, there were worse places to hang out. As much as she distrusted the kindness and generosity of these strangers, this adorable, partially furnished house with fresh white paint, trendy gray cabinets and stainless-steel appliances was more than she could've hoped for.

Her years in the military had afforded little time or energy for customizing her on-base housing into anything that felt like her own. She wasn't there much, anyway. And as a diver, she relished every opportunity to leave the ordinary world behind and submerge herself in the depths of the sea, devoted to fulfilling her orders. Completing the mission for the good of the order. Then she didn't have to think about how lonely her solitary existence had become, or how many thousands of miles stretched between her and her baby girl.

Unexpected emotion tightened her throat. She pushed her plate away, grabbed a cup and filled it with water from the kitchen sink. Gulping down a long sip, she mentally scratched and clawed for control. These people, Landon's family and friends, wanted her around. Or at least they behaved like they did.

You can stop running now. He can't hurt you anymore.

The thought was so ridiculous, so insane, that she sucked in a breath, which made her choke on her water. She wasn't *running*. A strong, independent woman didn't run. She stood firm. Protected her child. Like a good mother was supposed to. Being cautious did not mean she was pushing anyone away.

Was she?

The sound of the door sliding open sent a wave of panic sweeping through her. She gripped the edge of the counter. He couldn't see that she was battling back tears. Not again. If he saw her cry twice in two days, then he'd know his friends' and family's generosity had gotten to her. She couldn't have that.

"She fell asleep." His voice was low and soft. Buttery.

Kelsey squeezed her eyes shut and forced herself to think about obstacles she had conquered. Deep-water jumps. Swimming underwater until she thought her lungs might explode. Floating prone for five minutes— anything to make her feel the opposite of how she felt when she heard his voice. Anything to escape the reality that the same Landon she'd tried so hard to forget was back in her life, and she could no longer avoid the fact that they shared a child.

"Want me to put her down in the crib?"

"Yep." She opened her eyes but refused to turn around. Drawing a deep, calming breath, she silently willed Landon to carry Adeline down the hall. Instead, he hesitated. Her skin warmed as she sensed him watching her. She tightened her grip on the counter and battled back the urge to face him.

Stay strong. Don't let anyone see your weakness. They'll only use it against you.

The wisdom once offered by a seasoned officer echoed in her head. Except her heart refused to listen. Why didn't the advice she'd clung to in her military career translate to her personal life? Because inside, deep down, she longed to turn around. To risk being known. To have a partner. To be an essential part of an unbroken family.

Finally, Landon's boots clicked slowly down the hall to the bedroom with the crib. Kelsey sagged with relief, then quickly buzzed around the kitchen like a worker bee, diligently organizing the bounty of supplies piled on the counter. When Landon returned, she avoided eye contact and stayed in motion.

"Anything else I can help you with before I go?"

"Nope." She flashed him a polite smile. "I'm all set, thanks."

His brows tented. "Are you sure?"

"Absolutely." She stowed an extra roll of paper towels and a box of trash bags in the cabinet under the sink, then moved on to the plastic cups, utensils and paper plates. Wow, they'd thought of everything.

He lingered until she glanced at him over her shoulder. "Is there something else you wanted to discuss?"

Irritation flashed in his eyes. "No, I guess not."

She narrowed her gaze. Why was he annoyed? Oh, right. She had offered to share some of the food. Except sitting with him while he ate was the last thing she wanted to do. Too much opportunity for conversation. "Did you want to take some food with you?"

"No, thanks." He turned and ambled toward the door. "I'll see you tomorrow."

Kelsey opened her mouth to protest, then remembered she had a sleeping baby in the house and clamped her lips tight. She didn't have the energy to argue, anyway.

As the front door clicked shut, she slid to the floor

and hugged her knees to her chest. She did not need him to stop by and check on her. Or tell her what he thought was best for Adeline. Now that she had agreed to stay here, she'd hoped he would spend all his time working on the farm and leave her alone.

She tipped her head back against the kitchen cabinet and closed her eyes. This arrangement was the worst idea ever. They'd almost had an argument over a baby swing, so how would they ever agree on a care plan for Adeline?

Time was not on her side. She needed to act quickly. Tomorrow she'd call her mother and convince her to plan Wade and Maggie's memorial service ASAP. Folks here were sweet and thoughtful, but she wasn't going to spend another minute longer than she needed to in Merritt's Crossing.

Landon squinted into the golden sunlight splashing across the basketball court behind the elementary school on this late July morning. The well-loved ball glided across his fingertips as he took a shot. He leaned sideways, willing the ball to sink through the hoop. Instead, it clanked off the side of the metal rim then bounced on the pavement.

"That's an *S*," Gage called out, jogging after the ball.

No kidding. Landon scowled at his friend's back.

Gage retrieved the basketball then turned around, dribbling in between his legs, and grinned at Landon.

"Thanks for rubbing it in." Landon rested his hands on his hips. Man, he couldn't stand losing. Especially a game of H-O-R-S-E.

Gage chuckled then took a giant step toward the hoop. "I'll go easy on you."

Landon bit back another snide remark. That was the problem. He didn't want anyone to go easy on him. He wanted to win, especially since the rest of the guys would show up in a few minutes for an intense pickup game of five on five. Having to leave and slink to his truck while everyone else stayed and played was humiliating. Losing three straight to Gage only piled on the shame. His back would never tolerate the running, pounding and the quick change of direction from a full-court game of basketball, but he hated sitting on the sidelines almost as much as he hated losing another game of H-O-R-S-E.

With kids and teachers on summer vacation, Gage, Landon and a dozen other local guys met twice a week to use the vacant court. The sound of the ball bouncing at Gage's feet echoed off the one-story school building nearby. Gage dribbled back and forth between his left and right hands, eyeing Landon.

"You're not quite your cheerful self this morning. Something on your mind?"

"I need to convince Kelsey that Adeline stays with me."

Whoa, okay. That sounded just as ridiculous out loud as it did in his head.

Gage scooped up the ball and trapped it against his torso. "Do you mean overnight? On weekends? Every other week—"

"I mean permanently. Once Kelsey goes back to Hawaii, I want Adeline to stay with me."

Gage's brows lifted. "How do you think she'll respond when you ask?"

"She'll say no." Landon kicked at a pebble on the pavement and sent it careening into the grass at the edge of the court. "That's why I need your help. Do you know anything about parenting plans or family plans and how all that works when one parent is enlisted?"

"She's probably required to submit a family care plan to her commanding officer."

"That's what she told me—something about proof that her child was being cared for properly so she could fulfill her commitment to the navy."

"And you feel you can provide Adeline with the love and care she needs?"

"Of course. I'm her father." Landon glared at him. "And I'm a much better option than Kelsey's mother and stepfather."

Gage held up one palm. "Easy. No judgment here. I'm on a fact-finding mission."

"Sorry," Landon grumbled. "This whole thing has me all torn up."

"I get it." Gage shifted his weight from one foot to the other. "Skye and I had a rough time sorting out all the details about Connor's care. When does Kelsey plan on separating from the navy?"

"Next October."

Gage launched an effortless jump shot. The ball arced through the air, then slid through the net. "Fifteen months is a long time to be a single dad."

"I'm going to be a single dad for a lot longer than that." Landon retrieved the ball and moved toward Gage's position on the court. "Kelsey and I aren't together."

Gage stepped out of the way so Landon could mirror his position. "Not yet, anyway."

"Ha. Not ever again." Landon aimed for the faded

square on the scuffed metal backboard. "She can't stand me."

"And yet, you're both here. Living less than two miles apart with an adorable baby girl forcing you to bond."

That last comment really got under his skin and trampled all over his confidence. He shot the ball then groaned as it collided with the front of the rim and ricocheted onto the court. It rolled across the pavement and bumped against the front tire of Gage's pickup truck parked nearby.

"*Forced* is a good word for it. The woman wants nothing to do with me."

"Give it time," Gage called over his shoulder, jogging toward his truck.

"Yeah, whatever." Landon trudged after him. When he missed that last shot, he'd added an *E* to his dismal score. Gage had beat him again.

Gage picked up the basketball. "You want some water?"

"Sure."

Gage opened the passenger door, set the basketball on the seat then pulled two bottles of water from the small cooler on the floorboards. He handed one to Landon then cracked the other open for himself.

"Thanks." Landon twisted the cap off and took a long sip. After he'd finished, he wiped his mouth on the sleeve of his T-shirt. "Now that Wade and Maggie are gone, Kelsey has to submit a new plan. I want to be Adeline's guardian. I deserve the opportunity."

"Hey, you don't have to convince me," Gage said. "I'm totally on your side. Did the navy give her a deadline?"

"Sixty days until she has to report back to base and submit her new plan."

He'd done everything he could think of to help Kelsey feel comfortable at Laramie's place. His friends and family had gone above and beyond the call of duty with food, household supplies and more than enough baby equipment to keep Adeline happy. He hadn't raised his voice or threatened to hire an attorney. So why had she behaved like a frightened, caged animal yesterday when he'd offered to stay and help with Adeline?

"Skye and I couldn't agree on a plan at first, either." Gage twisted the cap back on the bottle. "Even though we both had the same goal—keeping Connor safe and healthy—we had completely different approaches."

"So you're trying to tell me all this conflict and tension is totally normal."

Gage grinned. "Exactly."

"How'd you finally agree?"

"I kept my promises, showed up on time and never gave her a single reason to doubt my commitment."

"Well, when you put it like that, this should be a breeze," Landon scoffed. "I mean, I don't even know why I'm worried."

Gage chuckled and clapped him on the shoulder. "You'll both figure this out. God's got this, by the way. He already knows what's best for all three of you."

"Right." Landon drained the rest of the water. He'd leaned hard on the Lord's promises over the last couple of years. While he wasn't about to turn from his faith now, the old familiar doubts were creeping in, like pests threatening to destroy a plentiful crop.

"Let us know if there's anything we can do to help."

"Thanks." The rumble of approaching vehicles kept him from saying more. "I've got to get going."

Understanding flashed in Gage's eyes. He knew Landon couldn't play five on five with the guys and that it tore him up to sit out. "See you around."

Landon's tired legs carried him toward his own vehicle. He wanted to leave before he had to struggle to make small talk with his friends. Or worse, had to pretend not to care that he couldn't join them. He threw a casual wave in the direction of the first car pulling in beside him, then slipped behind the wheel of his truck and drove away.

As he headed back to the farm, Gage's words echoed in his head. *Kept my promises, showed up on time and never gave her a single reason to doubt my commitment.*

There was only one small problem with those tidbits of wisdom. No matter what, Kelsey would never see him as trustworthy. She'd doubted him since day one. He had to find a way to rebuild what he'd shattered when he'd left her, pregnant and alone.

Chapter Six

Kelsey spread the striped blanket on the grassy area near the community park's playground, then sat down. Landon claimed the opposite corner and placed Adeline beside him. She immediately fussed, her smooth face wrinkling as she grabbed at the brim of the white sunhat Kelsey had put on her head.

"I brought some toys." Kelsey quickly opened the backpack they'd been using as a diaper bag and pulled out a vinyl book with pictures of jungle animals, her favorite shaker that sounded like rain when she tipped it on its end and the container of puffy rice snacks she often devoured.

Adeline ignored the toys and pushed out a few quick breaths, pointing toward the snack.

Landon chuckled. "Nothing wrong with a snack before playtime, right?"

Except she'd just eaten lunch before they left the house. Kelsey popped the lid off then passed him the container. He sprinkled a few onto the blanket.

"Oh." Kelsey grimaced. "How do you know this blanket's clean?"

Adeline's mouth formed an O as she grasped one of the puffs between her thumb and first finger then held it out for Landon.

"A little dirt never hurt." Landon rolled onto his side and propped up on one elbow, his long denim-clad legs stretched out in front of him. "That's what my mom always said."

Kelsey couldn't look away as he made a playful growling noise then pretended to bite Adeline's little hand.

Her adorable belly laugh nearly dissolved Kelsey into a puddle.

He was *so* good with her. So good that she almost felt guilty for doubting him and his ability to be the father Adeline needed.

Kelsey's phone pinged with an incoming text. She pulled it from the side of the diaper bag and glanced at the screen. Her commanding officer was checking in.

This is a reminder that you have 50 days to file a new care plan for your daughter. I hope you and your family are well. Please let me know if there's anything I can do to help facilitate this process.

She shoved the phone back in the bag without answering.

Landon studied her. "Everything okay?"

"Yep. Everything's peachy."

"That must be why you've got that groove between your eyebrows again."

What groove? She touched her finger to her forehead. There wasn't a groove.

Tipping her head back, she admired the white cotton-ball clouds dotting the blue sky. The midday sun warmed her skin. Adeline had taken a long morning nap, so when Landon asked if they could meet at the park after lunch, Kelsey felt confident saying yes. Sure, Adeline had resisted wearing her sun hat, but that was to be expected. Right? At least she and Landon hadn't argued. Yet. Why ruin a peaceful outing by discussing their daughter's future?

Guilt soon niggled at her. Even though she'd rather not mention the care plan, they didn't have the luxury of avoiding the subject forever.

"That was my commanding officer, reminding me the clock is ticking and I only have fifty days to submit my new care plan."

A muscle in Landon's jaw flexed. "Have you given any thought to your new plan?"

Kelsey picked at the clover blooming on the ground beside the blanket. "My mom and stepdad aren't capable of taking care of Adeline. Not yet, anyway."

"Realistically, probably not ever again."

Not ever? That hardly seemed accurate. Her stepdad's health might improve. She ignored his comment and tried a more pragmatic approach. "I know you think you can handle being a single dad, but you're busy, too. A farm is a huge responsibility and no place for—"

"We have help." Landon pushed into a sitting position. "My parents are healthy. Dad still does quite a bit, and he's teaching me everything I need to know to take over when he decides to retire. Most of our equipment runs by computer and GPS anyway, so farming is much more efficient than it used to be."

"But somebody else would have to take care of Adeline most of the time while you're…planting stuff."

His mouth twitched. "Is that what you think I do all day? Plant stuff?"

She sighed. Now was not the time for his jokes. "I have no idea what you do all day, but you don't seem like you have much free time to hang out with a baby."

"I'm hanging out now, aren't I?"

"And I'm trying to discuss our limited options, but I'm afraid we're going to argue."

"We're not arguing, we're having a conversation. I'm asking important questions about our daughter's future." He dipped his head and forced her to meet his gaze. "I'm not the enemy."

"Yet you want to keep our daughter in a situation that I'm not comfortable with."

Irritation sparked in Landon's eyes. Then he shook his head, stood and lifted Adeline into his arms. Adeline squealed and grabbed a fistful of his gray T-shirt. "I'm taking Adeline to try the swings. Don't worry, I won't let her fall on her head."

Kelsey stared after him, a snarky comment dying on her lips. He might not be her enemy, but they certainly weren't on the same team. Despite the heat of the summer day, a shiver of unease raced down her spine. This was an impossible scenario. She couldn't take Adeline to Hawaii, but she couldn't leave her here, either. Now that her family couldn't help, she didn't have any other reliable caregivers.

Lord, please help. I'm scared and confused.

Prayer hadn't come easily for her. A friend from her small group in Hawaii had shared that she'd struggled with prayer, especially since her relationship with her dad wasn't great, either. Kelsey appreciated the empathy, but empathy didn't solve her problems. What she needed was an answer. A defined plan that guaranteed Adeline's safety and security.

Was that too much to ask?

Landon double-checked the buckles on the blue-and-red plastic baby swing. "There. All good."

He gave Adeline's bare leg a gentle squeeze. Her hat had slipped off and fallen in the dirt under the swing. Oh well. A few minutes in the sun wouldn't hurt.

She jammed one finger in the side of her mouth and chewed on it, blinking her big blue eyes at him. Ack. She could have anything she wanted if she kept looking at him that way. Visions of buying her a pony filled his head. Didn't every little girl want her own horse at some point? He quickly squelched the notion. Kelsey would definitely raise a stink about that.

"Okay, baby girl. Hang on." He gave her a gentle push, staying in front of her the whole time. The breeze lifted a curl on the top of her head and she kicked her legs, obviously thrilled with her first outdoor swinging experience. She looked so adorable in her white shorts and baby-size pink T-shirt. He'd grab the hat as soon as he took a picture.

Pulling his phone from the back pocket of his jeans, he quickly snapped a photo. He shielded the screen from the sun, checked to make sure the picture was in focus, then snapped a few more and texted them to his parents. They didn't have any pictures of Adeline yet. He was trying to do better about sharing any that he captured.

"Are you sure she's buckled?" Kelsey's impatient tone jumped on his last nerve. "What happened to her hat?"

Landon tucked his phone away. "You slathered about a gallon of sunscreen on her. I'm sure she's fine."

"Not on her head. She has to wear her hat."

Oh boy. He stopped the swing, retrieved the hat and put it back on Adeline's head.

She shrieked and tried to push the hat off.

Great. Just great. Father of the year right here. "I know you hate it, but your mom says we have to."

"You don't need to make me the bad person. Do you want your baby to have a sunburn?"

"No, of course not." Did she think he was a monster? Adeline cried louder, kicking both legs in anger, and shoved the hat off her head.

"See? This is a perfect example of why I can't trust you. How could I possibly agree to you keeping Adeline while I'm thousands of miles away when you can't even keep a hat on her head to protect her from the sun?"

Ouch. He pushed his hands through his hair and turned away, forcing himself to take a few long strides and count to five before he answered. Her harsh words pierced him. The last thing he wanted to do was fire back with hurtful words he'd regret later.

"We're leaving."

Landon turned around, but Kelsey didn't wait for him to respond. Her fingers trembled as she unbuckled the swing then lifted Adeline into her arms. She strode across the small park, snatched her diaper bag off the ground, then slung it over her shoulder. When she tried to lean down and yank the blanket from the ground, she wobbled off balance, and Landon jogged to catch up.

She recovered, draped the blanket over her arm and strode toward the car. Adeline's pitiful crying filled the air. He jogged faster toward Kelsey's retreating backside. He couldn't let her go without at least defending himself.

He reached her car before she did and opened the back door. "No matter what you think of me, I'm still her father. I've never done this before, so I'm figuring things out as I go along. When I make a mistake, I try again. It's not a big deal."

She froze beside the open car door, Adeline wedged on her hip. "Not a big deal? This is a child. An innocent, helpless baby. You can't afford to make stupid mistakes, because then she'll get hurt."

"I would never hurt her on purpose." Landon fought to keep his voice even. "And no matter how hard you try, you're going to mess up sometimes, too."

"Not if I can help it."

Kelsey shoved the blanket onto the floorboard and tossed the diaper bag on top.

Man, for a girl who said she didn't want to argue, Kelsey sure knew how to land a powerful punch with her words. While she leaned into the car and put Adeline in her car seat, Landon stood back, his mind racing. Sweat trickled down his back, making his T-shirt stick to his skin. Spots peppered his vision. The temptation to retaliate with pointed words of his own was getting harder and harder to resist.

Kelsey straightened, then closed the door and faced him. "I'm not backing down. I can't go back to Hawaii not knowing whether she's safe."

"Can I ask you a question? Do you honestly think Wade and Maggie did everything perfectly? They didn't have children yet, so how do you know they didn't make mistakes while they were responsible for Adeline?"

She glared at him, her fists shoved on her hips. A

tense silence filled the space between them. "I didn't have to worry because Wade and Maggie weren't addicted to pills."

Anger burned white-hot. He opened his mouth, then clamped it shut.

She turned away, circled around the front of the car and climbed in without looking at him or even bothering to say goodbye.

He leaned down, grabbed a stone from the pavement at his feet and hurled it across the playground. Then he found three more and threw those, too. The rocks clinked against the metal frame of the play structure then fell to the ground.

Infuriating, that's what she was. When would she stop flinging his mistakes in his face? Worse, was she always going to use them as a reason to keep him away from Adeline? He hated that it had come to this. Maybe he'd have to hire an attorney after all, because she'd made her intentions clear. She wasn't going to let him keep Adeline.

"August tenth?" Kelsey reined in the irritation creeping into her voice. "That's two weeks from now. Why can't we have the memorial service sooner?"

Her mother sighed into the phone. "Maggie's mom had back surgery a month ago, and she's had some setbacks with her rehab. Now that she's lost her daughter, you can only imagine what a tough time she's having, and your father's still recovering from his episode."

"His episode? Is that the stroke you forgot to tell me about?" Kelsey sandwiched the phone to her ear while she collected the toys strewn across the living room floor. "I can't believe I had to find out about that from Landon."

"I didn't want to upset you. You have an important job to do."

"I also have a right to know what's going on at home." Kelsey squeezed the plastic rattle in her hand until her fingernails dug into her palms, then forced herself to take a deep breath. The news that Maggie and Wade's memorial service had been postponed made her want to fling the toy against the wall. "My stepfather had a stroke and you handed my daughter over to a total stranger. Those are two key facts you should've shared with me immediately."

"Landon Chambers is Wade's best friend. I'd hardly call him a stranger. We've had a rough month, honey. What with Wade and Maggie passing so suddenly and—"

"All the more reason for you to keep me informed, Mom."

"I was worried about sharing too much bad news all at once. You're alone and so far away, with nobody to lean on for support."

Oh, here we go. The if-only-you-had-a-man speech. "Please don't."

"Don't what?"

"Make me feel guilty for being an independent woman with a career."

"I am not making you feel guilty." Her mother's voice wobbled. "Your job is important. And so is your daughter. Adeline needs stability."

Oh brother. Kelsey massaged her forehead with her fingertips. Had Landon asked her to deliver this lecture? It sounded awfully familiar.

"I'm worried you won't be able to provide that for her," her mother continued.

Kelsey regretted making this phone call more and more with each passing second. No matter what they discussed, her mother always found a way to remind Kelsey that she should find a husband. That somehow her life was lacking because she didn't have that special someone. They'd been on this conversational merry-go-round countless times. Frankly, it was exhausting.

"Landon is so nice and so concerned about Adeline."

"He's also an addict."

"Everyone makes mistakes," her mother said quietly. "Adeline deserves to have her mother *and* her father in her life."

"Landon and I are not together," Kelsey said. "So please don't get your hopes up, because that's never going to happen."

Again. That's never going to happen *again*. She and Landon might be in the same zip code with their daughter, but it was only temporary. Falling in love with him was out of the question.

"I need to go."

Kelsey winced at her mother's wounded tone. "Mom—"

"Thank you for calling. Let me know when you're coming, and I'll get the guest room ready for you and Adeline."

"Okay, thanks." Kelsey ended the call and slumped on the sofa, staring at her phone in her hand. "So that went well," she whispered. Why didn't her mother accept any responsibility for her mistakes? She hadn't even apologized for asking Landon to take Adeline without permission.

Kelsey refused to support the skewed philosophy that a woman needed a man to be happy. That had always been her mother's approach. After she and Kelsey's father divorced, her mother hadn't been single more than a month before she found a new boyfriend. While none of the men who came and went from Kelsey's life ever harmed her, she had learned quickly not to trust. Not to get attached. Because they'd always leave. Eventually they'd choose something or someone else. Just like her father had.

Finally, after a long run of casual, failed relationships, her mother met and married Bill. Still, Kelsey never allowed herself to genuinely love him. As soon as she was old enough, she had enlisted and left home.

And now here she was, almost twelve years later, a single mom with a young daughter in need of a safe, stable home. She'd tried so hard to learn from her parents' mistakes. Tried so hard to make wise decisions. Tried so hard not to need anyone.

But her mother had been right about one thing. Adeline deserved to have her mother and her father in her life. And despite her intentions to keep Landon at arm's length, this news from her mother meant her stay in Merritt's Crossing was extended another week. Unless she convinced Landon that she and Adeline needed to travel to Wyoming without him.

Landon is so nice.

She batted away the words like a baseball player swinging for the fences. A nice guy wasn't enough. She'd seen plenty of nice guys leave. Or turn not so nice when life got too difficult to handle.

Except Kelsey couldn't ignore the nagging thought that her mom had been right about Landon. He was nice.

Kind and thoughtful, too. That smile might possibly be her undoing. Along with the scruffy five o'clock shadow hugging his jaw like it was its job.

Ugh. *Stop.* He was also a drug addict.

Kelsey slid her phone onto Laramie's rustic, distressed wooden coffee table, then stood and padded toward the kitchen. She paused, studying the closed bedroom door down the hall. Without a baby monitor, she had to rely on listening for Adeline to cry out when she woke up from her nap. So far, only the hum of the refrigerator nearby filled the air.

Kelsey checked the time on the microwave. Four fifteen. Adeline was sleeping longer than she had yesterday, but that was probably normal.

Wasn't it? She gnawed on her thumbnail, unsettled by the weighty responsibility of making decisions about her daughter all by herself.

It doesn't have to be this way, the quiet voice inside gently prodded her. *Landon is more than happy to help. You just have to ask.*

Wow, her mother had really gotten inside her head. Kelsey whirled away from the counter. She wasn't about to wake a sleeping baby. Everybody knew that was a bad idea.

Restless and bothered by her mother's words still flitting through her head, Kelsey opened the refrigerator and removed the casserole she'd defrosted for dinner. It was too much food for one person.

Maybe she could share a few bites of the casserole with Adeline if it didn't have too much garlic and onion. While she waited for the oven to preheat, she remembered a bag of precut broccoli someone had brought her and she pulled it from the fridge, too. This was so strange, living in someone else's house and using random pots and pans Landon's friends and family had donated. The kindness and generosity made her uncomfortable if she thought about it too much, so she focused on filling a pan with water to steam the broccoli.

The rumble of an approaching vehicle outside caught her attention. She glanced out the window above the kitchen sink. Landon. She recognized his white truck, along with the familiar way her heart kicked against her chest wall, like a horse eager to bolt from its stable and run free.

Settle down.

His truck churned up dust as he pulled into the gravel driveway.

He parked and climbed out of the cab. Her eyes homed in on his long denim-clad legs and lace-up brown work boots hitting the ground. Then he reached back into the truck and pulled out a plastic shopping bag. As he closed the door, a lock of his sandy-blond hair spilled over his forehead. He wore a navy blue T-shirt that rippled in the breeze as he walked toward the porch.

She couldn't look away. Her eyes followed him until cool water overflowed the edge of the pot then splashed in the stainless-steel sink.

Uh-oh. Good thing he hadn't caught her staring. She turned off the water, drained the excess from the pot, then set it on top of the stove. *This is not a big deal. He's allowed to stop by and see his daughter. There's no need to get all worked up.*

Her silent pep talk did nothing to calm her internal turmoil. Landon knocked softly at the front door, and she hesitated. She'd have to tell him about the new date for Maggie and Wade's memorial service—if her mother hadn't already let him know. He'd probably be thrilled to hear that she had a reason to spend another week in Merritt's Crossing.

She was the opposite of thrilled.

Drawing a wobbly breath, she crossed the room and opened the front door. Landon grinned and held up the plastic bag. "I brought you something."

His breath caught as her fingertips brushed across his knuckles.

"Thanks." Her gaze bounced away from his. He tried not to stare at her long lashes resting against her creamy cheek. Or her bare legs peeking out from the hem of her long sundress.

After their contentious meeting at the park yesterday, he'd planned on stopping by long enough to deliver the new baby monitor and hopefully spend a few minutes with Adeline.

Except he wasn't prepared for the magnetic pull drawing him toward Kelsey, making him wish she'd invite him in. Maybe even let him stay for dinner?

"What's this?" She pulled the cardboard box from the bag and examined it.

"It's a baby monitor. I thought you might need one."

She clutched the box in both hands then flipped it over and looked at the back. Her mouth tipped up in a hesitant smile. "This is perfect. Thank you."

"You're welcome." Her bright expression grabbed ahold of him, and he felt like his legs were full of helium. When she turned that radiant smile his way, he almost believed he could fly.

Her smile quickly slid off her face. "How much do I owe you?"

"You don't owe me anything, Kels. I'm just trying to help. Make your life easier."

Her brows scrunched together. Probably measuring his response and trying to decipher any ulterior motives.

He patiently tucked his hands in the back pockets of his jeans, refusing to let her suspicion get to him.

Kelsey clutched the box to her chest. "Adeline's still asleep, but she'll probably wake up soon. Did you want to come in and say hi?"

Well, how about that. Maybe a spontaneous gift was the key to chipping away at the walls she'd constructed. He tried to mask his excitement. "Sure, I can hang for a few minutes."

Or an hour. Or three. She didn't need to know that all that waited for him at home was a frozen pizza and a professional baseball game on TV.

She stepped back and he went inside, then quietly closed the door behind him. As he followed her toward the kitchen, he couldn't help but admire how the lime-green cotton fabric of her dress emphasized her trim, athletic frame. He let his gaze rest on her long braid, intricately woven into a fishtail pattern he didn't see very often. Her hair was the color of burnished copper and spilled across her shoulder.

Maybe he should come back another time. A time when his hands weren't itching to play with the end of that braid, or twine one of those loose strands of hair that framed her face around his finger.

What in the world? Dude, get a grip.

Gage had recommended showing up and keeping

his word…not pulling her into his arms and kissing her senseless.

Heat crawled up his neck as he paused in the doorway, determined to keep a safe distance.

"Would you like something to drink? Water or iced tea? I think there's some lemonade, too."

Landon stared in disbelief as she moved around the kitchen. Why was she being so kind? So hospitable? Where was the feisty, fiercely independent Kelsey determined to keep him at arm's length no matter what?

"Water's fine. Thank you."

She set the monitor and shopping bag on the counter then filled a plastic cup with ice and added water. "Here you go." She handed it to him. This time he didn't let his fingers touch hers.

He took a sip of the water and stared at her over the rim of the cup.

She fired a curious look over her shoulder. "What?"

He leaned against the door frame, secretly enjoying that his presence couldn't be ignored. "Are you all right?"

"I'm fine. Why?"

"You're being really nice to me. It's unexpected, that's all."

Especially after yesterday.

She sliced through the packing tape with her fingernail, then opened the box. "You brought me something useful. The least I can do is offer you a glass of water."

"I see. So this hospitality is going to be short-lived, is that what you're saying?"

He caught the twitch of her lips as she turned away and tried to hide her smile. "You're not funny."

"I'm not? How about charming?"

She shook her head, extracted the owner's manual for the video monitor and spread it on the counter. He smothered a laugh then glanced around his sister's kitchen, which felt decidedly different now that Kelsey had moved in. While Laramie preferred a lot of homey touches and made her space quite feminine, Kelsey had gone for the minimalist look. Probably because she didn't have much, but even if she had moved in with all her own possessions, she struck him as an a-place-for-everything-and-everything-in-its-place kind of woman.

The sound of Adeline crying, muffled behind the closed bedroom door, caught his attention. "Want me to get her?"

"Wait."

He hesitated. Oh no. He'd only been here a few minutes. How had he messed up already?

Uncertainty lingered in her expression as her eyes met his. "I—I owe you an apology."

Huh. She was full of surprises today. "Go on."

"I'm sorry for the way I spoke to you yesterday at the park. Keeping Adeline from getting sunburned is important, but I should never have said those terrible things to you."

Landon swallowed hard. "Apology accepted."

She fidgeted with the paper on the counter, dog-earing a corner of the manual, then looked away. "Thank you."

"You're a great mom, Kelsey. Adeline is blessed to have such a loyal and devoted parent."

Her chin wobbled, and he braced against the door frame, shocked by her emotional reaction. Had no one ever complimented her parenting before?

Adeline cried louder.

"I'm trying," she whispered finally, then tipped her chin up and cleared her throat. "You'd better go get her."

"Sure thing." He moved toward her, set his glass on the counter, then pumped his fist in the air as he walked quickly down the short hallway. A genuine smile, a glass of water *and* an apology. Now she was going to let him hold his own child. Man, he was batting a thousand today.

He pushed open the door. "Hey, pretty girl."

Adeline sat in her crib, fat, pitiful tears sliding down her flushed cheeks. When she saw Landon through the crib rails, she stopped crying and offered him a slobbery, toothy grin.

He melted faster than an ice cream cone on a hot summer day. She had him wrapped around her chubby little finger already.

"What's going on, pumpkin?" He crossed the small bedroom then reached into the crib and picked Adeline up.

"Da, da, da," she cooed.

He couldn't move. Could barely breathe. He didn't want to do anything to ruin the moment. Was she about to say *dad*? Nah, couldn't be. Probably a coincidence. He couldn't resist coaxing her to say more, though.

"Adeline, can you say *daddy*?"

Her blue eyes widened as she studied him. Then she grabbed a fistful of his T-shirt in her hand and screeched. Right in his ear.

"Wow, you're a mess. We'd better get you cleaned up."

While he wasn't a fan of the slobber she was plastering on his shirt with her hand, the soggy state of her diaper and the back of her onesie seemed like a bigger problem. That and the fact she'd almost said *daddy*— probably before she'd said *mommy*. He had a feeling Kelsey would've gleefully reported that news the second he walked in the door.

"Girlfriend, I don't know a whole lot about diapers, but I'd say you've sprung a leak."

He scanned the room, looking for clean diapers and wipes. "Somebody really hooked you up, didn't they? Look at this. You've got a dresser for your clothes and a nice crib to sleep in. And check this out—someone even brought you a pink elephant. I didn't know elephants were pink."

He plucked the squishy stuffed animal from the top of the dresser then tapped it gently against her tummy. Adeline's bubbly laugh was just about the best sound he'd ever heard. Chuckling, he pulled the stuffed animal out of her reach, then slowly brought it back until she shrieked with delight.

"What does an elephant say? Do you know?"

Adeline squeezed the elephant with both hands then shoved one of its floppy ears in her mouth.

Boy, if his buddies from the bull riding circuit could see him now, they'd be doubled over with laughter. But he didn't care, because he'd do anything to make his baby girl happy.

Her enthusiasm over the elephant didn't buy him much time. She quickly dropped the toy and made a game of twisting out of Landon's grasp. After a few failed attempts and more than a little struggling, he finally got her diaper changed, and he even managed to put on a clean white onesie and a gray pair of pants. This outfit probably wasn't Kelsey approved, but he'd risk another critical glance rather than try to change

Adeline again. At least he was helping. That should count for something.

Holding Adeline carefully in his arms, he walked back out to the kitchen. The aroma of something delicious baking made his mouth water.

"This casserole is huge." Kelsey gestured toward the oven with her thumb. "Do you want to stay for dinner?"

Yes. No. "Sure, why not?"

Accepting her invitation meant a home-cooked meal and more time with Adeline. A win-win. But spending an evening with Kelsey was dicey and only reminded him of what he couldn't have—Adeline *and Kelsey* in his life. Together.

Chapter Seven

She never should've invited him to stay for dinner.

Kelsey scooped the remnants of the casserole into a disposable plastic container then sealed the lid. On the other side of the kitchen counter, Landon sat at the table holding Adeline on his lap. And looking way too good for a man who'd allegedly spent all day on the farm checking equipment, adding oil to engines or whatever farmers did to prepare for a wheat harvest. His broad shoulders, tan skin and the smile lines that appeared whenever Adeline made him chuckle invaded Kelsey's line of sight. She had no hope of resisting his charm if she didn't stop stealing covert glances.

Adeline's chatter filled the room as she babbled around the plastic measuring cup she'd been gnawing on for the past few minutes. Kelsey turned away and crossed the small kitchen to the refrigerator.

"Where did you hide all the desserts that people brought you?"

She hesitated, wedging the door open with her shoulder. Grateful for the cool air wafting toward her, she stalled, scrambling for an answer that didn't make her sound selfish or unappreciative. Probably a little late for that, though. And she wasn't going to lie to him. Not anymore.

"There are some brownies in the pantry." She closed the fridge and turned toward the sink. "I tossed everything else."

"You threw cookies away?" The teasing lilt in his voice did nothing to ease her guilt. "You'd better not let that news get out."

Ouch. He might be joking, but the words stung. She was an outsider here. They'd rolled out a generous welcome, but when she messed up and hurt Landon or didn't behave like they wanted her to, they'd turn on her in a second.

"I needed the containers for leftovers." Not to mention she had a uniform she'd have to fit in when she got back to Hawaii and a physical fitness evaluation to pass. Those stacks of cookies calling to her from the pantry shelves did not mesh well with her profession's expectations. She turned on the water then squirted dish detergent on the dirty plates stacked in the sink.

"Next time, share with me instead."

She fired an annoyed glance at him.

Unfazed, Landon grinned at her. "I'll trade cookies for plastic wrap and aluminum foil any day of the week."

"Noted." She washed sticky oatmeal from Adeline's red plastic bowl. She hadn't been a fan of the chicken and rice, so Kelsey fed her oatmeal, pureed pears and sweet potatoes instead.

"If there's anything you need, all you have to do is ask."

"I don't need anything." She refused to look at him.

Please, just go. But the silent plea wasn't effective. He stayed in his chair, the warmth of his gaze on her skin making her want to run for the hills. Instead of having a conversation like a mature adult, she did what she always did when conversations turned too intimate for her liking. She kept moving forward. A messy kitchen? Not a problem. She'd scrub until it shined.

Because if he kept treating her well and performing this father-of-the-year act, she was going to have to invent new and clever ways to resist him.

She had to protect her heart. She couldn't allow herself to fall for him again. He had a right to see Adeline, and he seemed committed to providing for his daughter, but that didn't mean Kelsey had to let him love her.

"Can I do anything to help before I go?" Landon offered.

"Nope, I got it." She squirted more detergent on the dinner plates. Why didn't he get the hint? She didn't want him in her space, making Adeline giggle, making life easier, making this house feel like a home and like they were a family.

That last idea sent panic ricocheting through her, and she dropped the slippery plate. It clattered in the sink, then cracked into three pieces. Adeline burst into tears. Kelsey gasped. Landon's chair scraped against the hardwood, and he was at her side in an instant.

"Are you okay?" His gentle hand on her shoulder made her spine straighten. Adeline's fussy cry pricked at her already-frayed nerves.

"I'm fine." She left the broken plate in the sink then turned and stretched out her arms toward Adeline. "I'll take her. It's time for her bath."

Crusty baby food clung to Adeline's cheeks, giving her round face an orange glow. Her high chair tray was coated in the stuff, and Kelsey spied some rice and chicken dried on the wall. Suddenly the bath, bottle and bedtime story routine loomed like a mountain she lacked the strength to summit.

Landon didn't relinquish his hold. "I can give her a bath."

The hopeful look in his eyes made her pause. He wanted to help. And bathing Adeline required patience she just didn't have tonight. "Okay. Go ahead. Do you know how?"

He hesitated. "Not exactly, but I can figure it out."

Don't be bossy. Let him try. The wisdom flitting through her head kept her from following him into the bathroom and monitoring his every move. That and Adeline's fussing indicated they needed to get her ready for bed.

"All right." She pointed toward the bathroom down the hall. "Baby shampoo and soap are on the counter. She uses the pink towel with the hood. It's on the back of the door. And don't take your eyes off her for even a second. Okay?"

"Use the shaving cream and the striped beach towel under the sink."

"What?" Did the man ever listen? "No."

He winked, sending her heart into a deep dive. "Just kidding."

Stinker. He was infuriatingly handsome, too.

While she finished cleaning up the kitchen, the sounds of splashing and Adeline's bubbly giggles punctuated with the occasional squeal filtered in from the bathroom. It tempted Kelsey to grab her phone and sneak in to snap some photos, but she resisted. Landon would see right through her cover and probably tease her about checking up on him. Or worse, they'd end up arguing like they did yesterday at the park over Adeline's hat.

By the time she'd fixed a warm bottle of formula for Adeline and selected a board book from their small collection in the living room, Landon walked in carrying a clean but sleepy baby. Her chest squeezed. He'd even put her into her yellow pajamas with the tiny pink flowers.

Adeline's face scrunched up when she saw the bottle in Kelsey's hand, and she kicked her leg impatiently against Landon's side.

"Hold on, pretty girl." Landon carefully supported her with both hands. "Let your mom get ready."

Kelsey crossed to the paisley-print sofa and settled in. Landon handed Adeline to her. She quickly tucked her in the crook of her arm, then gave her the bottle. While Adeline drank with both hands clutching the clear plastic like it was her lifeline, Kelsey breathed in the soothing lavender scent of Adeline's shampoo. Was there anything sweeter than holding a warm, clean, snuggly baby?

Landon hovered behind the sofa, twirling his key ring in a circle around his finger.

She studied him. "What's wrong?"

"Let me take you to dinner."

"No." She couldn't imagine a more dangerous threat to her plan for keeping him at arm's length.

"Once we start harvesting wheat, there isn't a lot of downtime. If a storm shows up in the forecast, we go even harder to get the wheat in while it's still dry. I want you to have a break from taking care of Adeline. Just—"

"I don't need a break. She's my daughter, and I've been away for five months. I want to take care of her."

"I'm not implying that you can't." He held up both palms in surrender. "Taking care of a baby is hard work, especially if there's no one to share the load with."

"You're here now, helping me out. You've helped every day since I got here."

"Right, but I won't be able to help you once the harvest starts. My folks will be busy, too. You're going to be on your own with Adeline for several days."

Several *days*? Surely he was joking. "It's fine. I'll be fine. I've got this."

His brows slid upward.

"Thanks for the vote of confidence." She stared up at him. "Why are you doing this? Why are you being so nice to me?"

Hurt flickered across his features. "Because I care about you and I want you to be happy."

Her mouth fell open.

"My mom can watch Adeline for a couple of hours tomorrow night so we can go to dinner."

"You've already planned this?"

"I made sure she was available before I asked you."

Kelsey tipped her head back against the sofa. Dinner out sounded nice. Adeline would be safe with Landon's mom. She was her grandmother. They should spend some time together to discuss the decisions looming before them. Because there'd be a lot of them.

"All right," Kelsey relented. "Dinner, but nothing else. We need to talk. No movies, no walks through the park, no fireworks—just dinner. I want to be back in time to give Adeline her bottle before bed."

His mouth twitched. "Noted."

She narrowed her gaze. He was mocking her again. "What time should I be ready?"

"Six fifteen?"

"Great. See you then."

"Good night."

He slipped out the front door and closed it quietly behind him.

She kissed Adeline's forehead as her baby girl's eyes drifted closed. "Why did I let your daddy talk me into that?"

He hadn't been this nervous since his final ride on an angry bull to win his last world championship. Landon wiped his sweaty palms across his jeans one at a time, then grabbed the steering wheel. He sneaked a glance at Kelsey riding in his truck's passenger seat. She smelled good—like the air after a light spring rain. Some women chose fragrances that overwhelmed his senses. Not Kelsey. And her hair was styled in loose curls that spilled past her bare shoulders in shiny waves. She looked incredible. Not only did he have clammy palms, but his fingers itched to reach across the console and twine his fingers through hers.

Dude. Chill. Out. So not a good way to start their evening—daydreaming about holding hands when she'd made her expectations crystal clear. This was a casual dinner. A night out after a grueling week full of heartache and disappointment.

Still, after her apology and the tender moment they'd shared in the kitchen yesterday, he couldn't help but hope—hope that maybe he and Kelsey might still have a shot at a future together. A shot at being a family.

"So what would you be doing for fun if you were in Hawaii right now?"

He had to say something to break the loaded silence hovering in the truck's cab. Had to have a conversation with her that redirected his thoughts from the wild trek they'd just taken.

"I don't…get out much," she said softly, shifting away from him to look out her window.

"Really?"

That didn't sound like the Kelsey he'd met at Wade and Maggie's wedding. Admittedly, spending a weekend together at a wedding did not make him an expert on her habits, but she'd struck him as adventurous. The high-energy type.

"Diving keeps me busy. When I'm on base, I try to exercise, see a few friends or go to church if I have the day off."

Wait. Church? He quickly stifled the doubt that popped into his head. Questioning her wasn't fair. Or helpful. While it surprised him to hear church was a priority in her life, he tucked that fact away to revisit later.

"How about surfing? I hear Hawaii's beaches are some of the best in the world for that."

She shook her head. "I spend a lot of time in the ocean already. Surfing doesn't really interest me. Too slow. I'm not good at sitting around waiting, especially for a wave."

"Huh. Imagine that."

She shot him a curious glance. "What's that supposed to mean?"

"Nothing." He couldn't stop the smile tugging at the corner of his mouth. "You haven't sat still for more than a few minutes since you got here. Unless you're sleep-

LOYAL READER
FREE BOOKS VOUCHER

YES! I Love Reading, please send me up to 4 FREE BOOKS and Free Mystery Gifts from the series I select.

Just write in "YES" on the dotted line below then return this card today and we'll send your free books & gifts asap!

➡ YES ⬅
‑ ‑ ‑ ‑ ‑

Which do you prefer?

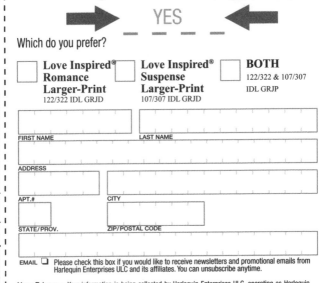

☐ **Love Inspired®
Romance
Larger-Print**
122/322 IDL GRJD

☐ **Love Inspired®
Suspense
Larger-Print**
107/307 IDL GRJD

☐ **BOTH**
122/322 & 107/307
IDL GRJP

FIRST NAME

LAST NAME

ADDRESS

APT.#

CITY

STATE/PROV.

ZIP/POSTAL CODE

EMAIL ☐   Please check this box if you would like to receive newsletters and promotional emails from Harlequin Enterprises ULC and its affiliates. You can unsubscribe anytime.

LI/SLI-520-LR21

ing or eating. I've never surfed, but I thought it might appeal to the side of you that appreciates a challenge."

"I have Adeline to think about. I can't afford to take senseless risks."

"Right." *Oh brother.* Hard to miss the subtext there. He'd been a bull rider who took more than his fair share of senseless risks. Maybe this was a bad idea. They couldn't even talk about the ocean without stumbling into a conflict.

He'd just wanted to do something nice. Something kind for her. She'd had her life completely turned upside down by the loss of her stepbrother. Worse, she'd had to come home unexpectedly and deal with him, care for her baby again, grieve and adjust to the news of her stepfather's declining health. Seemed like a lot for one person to handle all at once.

Maybe he'd underestimated her. Maybe she liked being on her own. While he sympathized with all she had going on, he still wasn't about to let her leave town and take Adeline. He couldn't stand the thought of not seeing his baby girl every day. They'd have to come to some sort of agreement. Maybe tonight could be the first step in forging a plan they could all live with.

He slowed down, turned into the parking lot and claimed the last remaining space in front of Pizza Etc. "Here we are."

She stared through the windshield without saying a word.

Lord, give me patience. He turned off the ignition. A hot, dry breeze greeted him as he climbed out of the truck, circled the front and opened the passenger door for her.

Kelsey didn't move.

"Looks busy." She frowned. "Is this where everyone hangs out?"

"Define everyone."

Her gaze swung to meet his. "Are all your friends here?"

"Probably." He shrugged, then offered her his hand. "Don't let that discourage you, though. I promise I'll behave."

She ignored his hand and slid to the ground, then slipped her purse over her shoulder.

He slammed the truck door, nearly pinching his finger as he caught a look at her.

While he'd most definitely be a gentleman tonight—and every night—he couldn't deny she looked amazing in her white sleeveless blouse, denim skirt and cowboy boots.

Gravel crunched under their boots as he led the way to the restaurant's entrance. Inside, a nineties country tune played on the jukebox in the corner. A few couples two-stepped around the dance floor.

She faced him with a look of panic in her eyes. "You said nothing about dancing."

He held up his hands. "No one's going to force you to dance. Relax. Let's grab dinner, all right?"

Doubt lingered in her expression, but he refused to let one harmless song on the jukebox derail their evening. "Would you like to choose where we sit? Looks like there's only two empty tables left."

She tipped her chin up then wove through the crowded dining room until she arrived at a small table for two on the far side—the farthest distance from the jukebox and the dancing couples.

Landon felt curious stares trailing them. He smiled

and waved to as many familiar faces as possible, although he nearly tripped over the toes of his own cowboy boots when he passed Drew Tomlinson sitting with a woman Landon didn't recognize. An intensely private person, Drew went to great lengths to keep his personal life away from the prying eyes of locals. Bringing a date into Pizza Etc. was a bold move on his part. Landon wanted to clap him on the shoulder or offer him a high five. Instead, Landon kept moving without making eye contact and joined Kelsey at the high top for two.

"Good choice," he said, sliding onto the tall, hard-backed chair across from her.

The vinyl cushions squeaked as he settled in and leaned forward, his elbows resting on the glossy, worn surface of the dark wood table. Kelsey hooked her purse strap over the back of her chair, then surveyed the crowded restaurant. "True or false. You can name every person in here right now."

Here we go again. Why did she care who saw them together? He swiveled in his seat and looked around the room. "Not quite. I'd say eighty percent."

Landon tried not to stare when the woman with Drew laughed and clasped her hand over his. *Would you look at that*, Landon silently mused. Good for Drew. He shifted his attention back to Kelsey. "Why do you ask?"

Before she could answer, Sienna, one of the regular waitresses, stopped at their table. "Hey, stranger." She grinned, her wide green eyes sweeping over Landon and making him uncomfortable. "Haven't seen you in a while. How've you been?"

"Good, thanks." Landon accepted the menu and studied it carefully. As if he didn't already have it memorized. Maybe if he kept his eyes on the laminated flyer, he could ignore Kelsey shooting him a pointed I-told-you-so stare.

"So what can I get you guys to drink?" Sienna pulled two paper coasters from the front of her black apron and set them on the table. "You know you're the hot topic around here, Mr. World Champion Bull Rider."

Sienna's megawatt smile and the way she leaned in close enough to let her bottle-blond hair brush his forearm made him want to drop his menu and leap out of his chair. Or clamp his hand over her mouth. Because he knew exactly where this line of questioning led.

"What's this I hear about a *baby*?"

Oh. No. Kelsey's sharp intake of breath and the toe of her boot colliding with his shin sent pain shooting through his leg.

"Why don't you give us a minute?" Landon forced a smile. "Kelsey's never been here before."

"No problem." Sienna winked and flounced away to her next table.

"I'm sorry." He countered Kelsey's simmering anger with a sincere apology. "We can go if you want."

He should've known better than to bring her here. One thoughtless comment from Sienna had unraveled all his progress. A quiet restaurant in the Denver suburbs where no one knew them would've been a far better choice. Once again, his thoughtless, impulsive behavior had forced Kelsey into an uncomfortable situation. Worse, it emphasized all the reasons why she didn't want to be part of a close-knit community.

Something told him intimacy scared her, and scared people were always the first to run. He would know. He'd been the first to flee whenever someone tried to get close.

* * *

She didn't mean to sound so uptight. Really, she didn't. But coming to this crowded restaurant where it felt like everyone was looking at her, and the waitress flirting shamelessly with Landon and getting all up in her business…well, it made her nervous. Annoyed. Worse, it reminded her of all the times people had gossiped about her father's scandalous behavior.

"No, it's fine." She pulled in a deep, calming breath. "We can stay."

"Are you sure?"

She nodded, then flipped the menu over and perused the rest of the limited options.

Another waitress came to their table to take their order—an older woman with salt-and-pepper hair twisted into a neat bun. Her kind eyes crinkled at the corners as she offered Kelsey a polite smile. "Sienna's on break. I'll be taking your order. What can I get for you, honey?"

The knot between Kelsey's shoulder blades loosened a smidge. "I'll have the Cobb salad, please. Honey mustard dressing on the side and a glass of iced tea."

"Excellent. And for you?" The woman turned toward Landon, her pen poised above her notepad. No obnoxious comments. No lingering stares. No flirtatious smiles. Maybe this place wasn't so bad.

"I'll have a cheeseburger, medium well, with cheddar cheese, fries and a Sprite, please."

"Of course." She took their menus. "We'll have that out shortly."

"See?" Landon said. "Not everyone who works here is collecting every detail of your life story."

"Good to know." Kelsey twisted her coaster in a circle and tried to pretend the teasing lilt in his voice and the mischievous gleam in his hazel eyes wasn't getting under her skin.

"It's probably none of my business, but—"

"But you're going to ask anyway," she finished his sentence. "Because you can't help yourself."

Landon's chuckle was easy and smooth—and reminiscent of the night they met.

Do. Not. Go. There, she silently warned herself, bracing for his question.

"What is it about small-town life that bothers you so much? If I recall, you're from Oklahoma. That's not Manhattan or LA or someplace super glamorous."

She tipped her head to one side. "Did you just insult Oklahoma?"

"My apologies to the fine, hardworking citizens of Oklahoma." His grin stretched wide across his tan face. "Now answer the question."

Kelsey studied him. He'd shaved and wore a short-sleeved pale blue button-down with dark-wash jeans and boots. She tried not to think about how it might feel to tunnel her fingers through his tousled blond hair. The current song playing through the speakers ended, replaced by the hum of conversation, laughter and silverware clinking against plates. Where to begin? And how to accurately convey her feelings to someone who clearly loved his hometown?

"I know you have a lot of respect for Wade and my family. They think highly of you, but my mom is a master at spinning things. Making situations seem better than they are. She conveniently leaves out key details and has never once acknowledged her role in my chaotic childhood."

Landon's expression grew serious. Those gold-flecked eyes bored into her, and she had to look away. "She moved us around a lot. My dad was a mess." Kelsey hesitated, uncertain how much to share. She forced herself to meet Landon's gaze. "My dad was an addict, and they got divorced but never stopped fighting over me. They passed me back and forth, but sometimes my dad didn't show up and I figured out quickly he wasn't trustworthy. I lost track of how many boyfriends she had before she met my stepfather. It seemed like everyone else had it all together, but I was always embarrassed and ashamed of my family."

Landon's brow furrowed. "People talked about you when you went to school. Whispered behind your back in the hallway. Exactly like they're doing right now."

Nailed it.

She managed a nod.

"Is that why the navy is so appealing?"

The same waitress returned with their drinks. Kelsey hesitated, waiting until she'd walked away before she answered.

"I know exactly what's expected of me." She peeled the paper wrapper off the straw then jammed it into her iced tea, poking at the crushed ice floating near the surface. "The assignments are challenging. I work hard, and I don't quit until the mission's accomplished."

"And then you're off to your next dive, new orders in a new location. You don't stick around long enough to be known. To let people in."

She froze, her glass halfway to her mouth. "That is not fair."

"But I'm not wrong."

Landon's expression reflected empathy. His tone was

gentle. But his words prodded at a wound she'd tried to pretend had healed. And she didn't like it. Not one bit.

She set her glass down, slid to her feet and yanked her purse off the chair. "I can't do this."

"Kelsey, wait."

Ignoring Landon's plea, she wove through the tables, her skin flushed and legs trembling. This was a mistake, letting him talk her into dinner. Letting him convince her she deserved a night out, when all he really wanted to do was criticize how she lived her life. Probably to persuade her to let him keep Adeline. Permanently.

Pushing past the family coming into the restaurant, Kelsey strode outside and crossed the parking lot. In her rush to get away from Landon, she hadn't thought about how she'd get home. Stranded, she turned in a circle beside his stupid truck.

"Great. Now what?" she grumbled and tipped her head back, staring at the evening sky. Rich shades of orange and red spilled across the pale blue canvas. Clouds outlined in wispy pink brushstrokes floated on the horizon. The red lights on the wind turbines blinked in the distance.

"Kelsey, please." She turned, her nails biting into her palms as she clenched her fists at her sides.

Landon jogged toward her. He stopped inches away and shoved his hands on his hips. Confusion flitted across his face. "What happened?"

Heat blazed through her body. "Don't."

"Don't what?"

"Pretend like you know what's best for me." She fought to keep from raising her voice. "You have a long history of being a major screwup, Landon Chambers, so you have no right to tell me how to live my life."

Pain flashed in his eyes. A muscle in his jaw knotted tight. "I'll drive you home."

"Good."

He reached past her and opened the truck's passenger door.

She scooted by, carefully avoiding letting her arm or any other part of her body brush against him. Even though he'd made her mad enough to spit nails, she couldn't deny that his smile, his laugh and those gold-and-green eyes affected her. Which was incredibly foolish on her part, because he'd trounced all over their fragile peace with his judgy comments.

No matter how good he looked or how well he cared for Adeline, she was better off without him in her life. Little girls needed a trustworthy father. Not some cowboy who'd break promises and leave. Just like her father had.

Chapter Eight

He'd barely eased his truck to a stop in front of his sister's house before Kelsey grabbed the door handle and hopped out of the cab.

Landon jammed the gearshift into Park, cut the engine, then hurried after her. "Kelsey, wait."

Man, he was saying that a lot lately. Tonight was not going at all how he'd planned. He wanted to make things right before she rushed inside and closed the door in his face.

While he expected her to ignore him like she had when she'd stormed out of Pizza Etc. a few minutes before, she surprised him by whirling around before her boots hit the porch.

"What?"

That terse, one-syllable response hinted at her barely contained anger. Her ramrod-straight spine and fierce glare warned him that he didn't have much time to plead his case. And here he thought they'd made progress. Somehow he'd managed to mess that all up before they'd even started their meal.

He stopped in the middle of the driveway, keeping

a safe distance, and cupped the back of his neck with his hand.

"Can we talk about this, please?"

"We just did. You ruined it by insulting me."

"What? I didn't *insult* you. I was trying to empathize."

An exasperated look that silently screamed *oh, please* flashed across her features. The breeze picked up, rippling her hair against her shoulders. Despite the tension arcing between them, his arms ached to hold her. Draw her close. Leave a trail of kisses along the curve of her jaw.

He banished the thoughts as quickly as they skidded through his mind, though, because she looked angry enough to spit fire.

"Huh," she said. "Which part was the empathy? When you judged me? Or maybe it was the part where you insulted my career? Wait, no. I bet it was the part where you criticized the way I live my life." She moved toward him slowly. Deliberately. Each click of her boot on Laramie's driveway landed like a punctuation mark.

Whoa. He opened his mouth to protest, but she wasn't finished.

"You have no idea how hard it is to be a single mother." She stopped in front of him, her eyes glittering, and jabbed her finger into his chest. "In fact, you know very little about me."

"That's where you're mistaken." He captured her hand, then pressed it over his heart, pinning her palm with his while he stepped closer. "I know that you love our baby girl with your whole heart. Otherwise you wouldn't have come here. I know that your parents hurt you. Deeply. I know that you're scared and that's why you run. Now you want to keep running because that's what's worked in the past."

Her chest heaved and her eyes widened, but she didn't pull away. "You can't charm your way out of this."

He caressed the back of her hand with the pad of his thumb. "Really?"

They were so close he could smell the tantalizing fragrance of her perfume.

"Yes, really."

"I don't believe you," he whispered, boldly stepping closer, leaving only a sliver of daylight between them. "You secretly find me incredibly charming. Maybe even irresistible."

His gaze slid to her lips—pink and slightly parted. Inviting him to kiss her. He let his eyes linger there, sensed her sharp intake of breath and relished the warmth of her hand still pressed over his heart.

"Wrong again, cowboy." She tugged her hand free. "You're only pretending to want me so you can have Adeline."

Ouch. "That is not true."

She turned and strode toward the porch. "Prove it."

Firing one more skeptical glare his direction, she climbed the steps and went inside.

Landon stared at the closed door. His mother deserved a proper thank-you for watching Adeline. He'd have to text her, because following Kelsey inside and continuing this conversation wasn't a smart move.

"All right, I will." He voiced his commitment into the empty yard. The lack of audience didn't dampen his resolve. He'd prove to Kelsey that he wanted her around because he cared about her, not because he was using her. He'd prove that even though people made mistakes, not all families treated each other like her parents had. Their relationship might not have started the right way, but he wasn't giving up. He'd show her they had something worth fighting for.

The next morning, Kelsey settled Adeline on the kitchen floor with a rainbow-colored shape sorter while she cleaned up the breakfast dishes.

"Da, da, da," Adeline jabbered while she banged a yellow plastic star against the edge of the cube-shaped sorter.

"Oh, let's not talk about him right now, okay?"

Adeline held up the star, then grinned and said, "Da, da, da, da, da."

Only louder.

Kelsey forced a weak smile then turned toward the sink, determined to forget last night's encounter with Landon. What a disaster.

He'd made her so mad. She should've known he wouldn't keep the focus of their evening centered on Adeline. When he'd shared those observations about her life, she'd felt exposed. Like she was standing on the side of the interstate holding a big sign that said B-R-O-K-E-N.

She wasn't broken, thank you very much.

Landon should've kept his opinions to himself. She ran warm water into the sink then added a generous squirt of dish detergent. How ironic. The injured, recovering addict trying to tell her how to be better at relationships. She'd tried to push back. Stand up for herself. But then he had to go and touch her. When he'd pressed her hand to his muscular chest and she'd felt his heart thrumming against her palm, all the snarky comebacks evaporated.

Then he'd almost kissed her. Worse, she'd kind of wanted him to. Not that she'd admit that to him. Ever. To be honest, when those gold-flecked eyes of his lingered on her lips, she'd nearly pushed up on her toes and kissed him first.

But then she'd come to her senses and put some much-needed distance between them. Because she'd remembered Adeline. Remembered all the times her father hadn't shown up when he was supposed to. Remembered how he'd blame her mother when he got caught lying about his drug use.

Her baby girl deserved a better life. That was why she had to come up with a new care plan. One that kept Adeline safe. Everything she'd done was for her. Even though Landon had the right to be a part of his daughter's life, that didn't mean she had to be in a relationship with him.

Last night had been a close call. She'd almost slipped. Forgotten how easily that half smile of his could send her defenses tumbling.

Doesn't Landon deserve a shot at proving he's changed?

Kelsey scraped at the dried egg stuck to the skillet with her fingernail, determined to ignore the voice of reason that had shown up uninvited.

Everyone makes mistakes. How long are you going to keep punishing him?

She wasn't punishing Landon.

Was she?

Uncertainty hovered as a knock at the door interrupted her thoughts. Kelsey dried her hands on a towel and peeked out the window over the sink. An unfamiliar blue minivan sat parked in the driveway. She wasn't expecting anyone, but then again, people around here seemed to drop by unannounced all the time. Adeline squealed and banged two shapes together. Her purple T-shirt was soaked already.

"Poor thing. You must be teething again." Kelsey picked up Adeline and wedged her on her hip. "Let's see who's here."

When she opened the door, a tall, dark-haired woman peeked out from behind a large bouquet of flowers wrapped in tissue paper and plastic. "Hi, Kelsey?"

"Yes?"

"I'm Skye Westbrook." She flashed a wide smile. "I think you've met my brother Drew already. Our family runs the furniture store in town."

"It's nice to meet you." Uncertainty prickled at her. She hadn't ordered any furniture. Or flowers.

"Landon asked me to deliver these. Aren't they gorgeous?"

Her mouth went dry. The yellow, purple and orange blossoms were mixed with rich green leafy things. She'd never been good at naming flowers, but she recognized at least half a dozen roses.

Skye's smile faded. "Are you all right?"

Adeline squealed and thrust her plastic star toward Skye, saving Kelsey from having to answer.

"You must be Adeline." Skye reached out and gave Adeline's bare leg a gentle squeeze. "My goodness, you are a beautiful girl."

"Thank you." Kelsey remembered her manners. "Would you like to come in for a minute?"

"Sure." Skye picked up a yellow gift bag resting at

her feet. "I brought you this, and I'd be happy to put these flowers in water for you."

"Oh." Kelsey looped her fingers through the bag's handles. "You didn't have to bring me anything."

"I know." Skye smiled again. "I wanted to."

"I'm not sure I have a vase." Kelsey stepped back and let Skye inside, then closed the door behind her.

"Oh, I bet I can find one. Laramie and I have been best friends for years. She married my brother, and I know for a fact he didn't let her bring everything she owned into his house. There's probably one on the shelf in the laundry room."

Really? Kelsey kept her grumpy comment from slipping out and transferred Adeline to her other hip. These people knew entirely too much about each other's lives.

"Looks like you're getting settled," Skye called over her shoulder as she set the flowers on the counter in the kitchen then moved toward the laundry room. "Do you like staying here? Laramie had everything all fixed up for a renter, then the girl backed out at the last minute."

Skye kept chatting away, her voice muffled as she stepped out of sight. She reappeared a minute later, a tall glass vase in hand. "Found one."

"Great." Kelsey swayed from one foot to the other, trying to soothe a wiggly Adeline.

"I'm happy to put the flowers in water while I'm here." Skye hesitated. "Unless you'd like to do it yourself?"

Adeline grabbed a fistful of Kelsey's hair and tried to shove her hand in her mouth.

"Ow." Kelsey flinched then gently extracted her hair from the baby's grip. "You can handle the flowers."

"Why don't you open your gift?"

"Right." Kelsey set Adeline on the kitchen floor. She scooted away on her bottom and grabbed the shape sorter with a victorious shriek.

"Oh, you are the cutest thing," Skye cooed at Adeline. "How long has she been scooting around like that?"

"This is the first time."

"Really?" Skye filled the vase with water. "You'll have to take a picture or a quick video. Landon will get a kick out of that."

"Yeah, I should."

Except documenting Adeline's milestones only reminded her of how much she'd missed during her deployment. Sure, Wade and Maggie had sent photos. Mostly they'd used FaceTime to keep in touch so Kelsey could see Adeline on screen. She was changing so quickly, though. What else would she miss when she had to go back to Hawaii?

A wave of regret washed over her, and Kelsey quickly shifted her focus back to the bag in her hand. She reached inside, pushed past the white tissue paper then pulled out a pink shirt and matching pink-and-white-striped leggings. They looked perfect for Adeline.

"These are adorable." Kelsey couldn't help but smile. "Thank you very much."

"You're welcome." Skye glanced up from tucking flowers into the vase. "There's one more thing in there for you."

Kelsey peeked inside the bag then pulled out a leather journal. She cracked the cover and flipped through the pages. There was a Bible verse, a few short paragraphs and blank lines on every page.

"It's a journal and a devotional, all in one. I thought

you'd enjoy having something that's just for you, especially since everybody's bringing you baby stuff and meals." Skye's blue eyes gleamed. "Well, except for Landon."

Warmth climbed Kelsey's neck.

"He told me to get the biggest bouquet the flower shop had, by the way. I've never seen him this devoted to anyone. You and Adeline are blessed to have him."

Kelsey couldn't stop the cynical laugh that bubbled up. "Are you sure we're talking about the same Landon?"

Skye's expression melted into one of confusion. "Uh-oh. What happened?"

"Nothing. It's…nothing. Never mind." Kelsey clamped her mouth shut. Yikes, she'd said too much. Skye was obviously Team Landon all the way. "I need to get Adeline down for her morning nap. Thanks again for the gifts."

"Of course." Skye's smooth brow furrowed. She tucked the last rose in the vase and dried her hands on a towel. "Let me know if you need anything else."

"I will." She set the clothes and the journal on the counter, then picked Adeline up and carried her into the bedroom. Thankfully, Skye took the hint, and a few minutes later the front door closed.

Now you want to keep running because that's what's worked in the past.

Landon's words resurfaced. Kelsey mentally shoved them aside as she changed Adeline's diaper. Using her common sense and discernment didn't mean she was running. Landon had hurt her deeply when he left her alone in that hotel room. She was supposed to work toward forgiveness, but that didn't mean she had to forget.

Right?

And as Adeline's mother, she couldn't overlook his past.

Sure, people here had been kind. This house, the baby gear, even Skye's gift all showcased the generosity of Landon's friends and family. But there wasn't a bouquet of flowers large enough to silence the warning bells clanging in her head. She couldn't risk trusting him again.

He couldn't wait another day to see her.

Three days had passed since he'd seen Kelsey, and almost four since he'd spent any quality time with Adeline. Every part of his body ached with fatigue as he climbed down from the combine. Streaks of pink and purple colored the evening sky. He limped across the dusty driveway toward his truck. They'd harvested four hundred acres of wheat and still had another four hundred to go. The weather forecast looked great for the next week, so they'd decided to stop for the night.

Pain ricocheted up his spine every time his work boots struck the ground. All he really wanted was dinner, a hot shower and a good night's sleep. Except he couldn't let another day go by without speaking to Kelsey. Not after the way their conversation had ended the other night. He'd texted twice to check on her this week. She'd responded with one- or two-word answers. If he hurried, he could get over to Laramie's house before Kelsey put Adeline to bed.

The lights were on in his parents' house as he walked by. Through the window he glimpsed his mom moving about in the kitchen. Probably fixing a late meal for Dad. Landon faltered. If he stopped by, she'd happily feed him. It was hard to resist his mom's cooking.

Except he had food at home. And while his parents wouldn't turn him away, he shouldn't drop in. Being a dad meant putting the needs of others before his own, right? Adeline needed to spend at least a few minutes with him. While he'd asked people to check in on Kelsey and Adeline during the harvest, he didn't want them to be his substitute. Putting off a meal for another hour wouldn't hurt. Besides, seeing Adeline and getting to hold her would be worth it. And if he was honest, seeing Kelsey would be a bright spot in his grueling day.

The thought tugged his mouth into a smile. He'd spent plenty of time thinking about her while he drove the combine. Yesterday he'd switched roles with Cal, one of the workers his dad had hired, and driven the semitruck to the grain elevator. Images of Kelsey had dominated his thoughts. Man, she was beautiful. Even in her feisty moments.

When he got to his truck, he pulled open the door and grabbed a clean T-shirt he'd stashed in the back seat. Once he'd changed and tossed his filthy shirt onto the passenger side, he climbed into the cab. Squeezing his eyes shut against the pain shooting down his leg, he leaned his head against the back of the seat. What he wouldn't give for a single dose of OxyContin right now.

Memories of the little white pills resurfaced. Taunting. Teasing. Just one, that was all he needed. A little something to take the edge off so he could get up tomorrow and do this all over again. He'd tucked three pills away, buried them in his glove compartment, in case the longing ever became unbearable.

No. He opened his eyes, gripped the steering wheel

and cranked the engine. He wouldn't give in. Temptation had attacked countless times, like an angry spectator jeering from the crowd, and he'd been able to power through. Plenty of other injuries had provoked pain far worse than this. He could handle it.

He *had* to handle it.

Because he wasn't about to backslide into using again.

Past experience had taught him that he couldn't conquer his cravings on his own, though. He had several strategies for coping, and he'd need every single one to get through this intense week. His next meeting with his sponsor was still two weeks out. Although he could call him anytime.

While he drove the short distance to Laramie's house, he silently prayed for strength. Relief from the chronic pain would be nice, too. He'd learned to cry out to the Lord for help when his addiction clawed at him. He hated feeling weak, but he hated failure even more. He didn't want to disappoint Kelsey. Not again.

He slowed down, clicked on his blinker then turned into Laramie's driveway. His headlights cut through the dusky evening and bounced across the back of Kelsey's rental car. At least she was home. Now—to convince her to speak to him and hopefully let him inside for a few minutes.

His pain hadn't subsided, but the anxious feelings of teetering on the edge of temptation had lessened some. And he didn't feel quite so out of control.

Through the living room window, he saw Kelsey get up from the couch with Adeline in her arms. The lamplight silhouetted her figure. He wanted to get to the door before she put Adeline in her crib.

He cut long strides toward the porch, flinching as his weary body protested. He climbed the steps and knocked softly on the door.

"Please open up," he whispered. Man, he really wanted to see his girls. *His girls.* What would Kelsey think if she heard him say that?

The dead bolt shifted, then the door opened slowly and Kelsey appeared on the other side. Adeline spotted him and offered a sleepy grin, kicking her leg against Kelsey's hip. His heart rocketed into orbit. This was his whole world. Right here.

"Hey." Kelsey's smile didn't quite reach her eyes. "This is a nice surprise. I figured you'd be asleep already."

"I stopped by to see how my gir—to see how you were doing. Is that all right?"

She hesitated, then nodded. "I'm getting ready to give Adeline her bottle."

"I'll do it."

"All right." She stepped back and pulled the door open. "Come on in."

Adeline cooed and stretched both her arms toward him.

"Hey, pretty girl." He glanced at Kelsey for permission. "Can I hold her?"

Kelsey handed her over. "I'll get the bottle."

Landon carried Adeline toward the couch, then slowly sank into the cushions. Settling her carefully on his lap, he breathed in her sweet, clean smell. Her yellow-and-white-flowered pajamas were soft against his calloused hands. She popped her thumb in her mouth and stared at him with those wide blue eyes. If this was his reward for long days in the dusty fields, he'd take it.

"What did you do today?" He gently bounced his knee up and down. "Give your mom a hard time? Rearrange all the pots and pans in the kitchen?"

She gave him another one of those sleepy, adorable smiles. What he wouldn't give for more evenings spent exactly like this. He and Kelsey, together, with their daughter. Building a life. Maybe even growing their family? Of course that meant marriage and Kelsey returning to Merritt's Crossing after she separated from the navy, two major life changes that seemed next to impossible at this point. Still, he stubbornly clung to the hope that he'd win her over.

Kelsey returned with the bottle.

Adeline saw it, and her expression crumpled as she fussed impatiently.

"Easy there." Landon shifted her into the crook of his arm, took the bottle and offered it to her. She clutched it with both of her tiny hands and started drinking. As she settled against him, he forgot all about his pain and fatigue for a few minutes and soaked in the contentment of holding his daughter close.

"How was your day?" He shifted his focus to Kelsey as she sat down on the opposite end of the couch and folded her tan legs underneath her. In her navy blue shorts, white-and-blue-striped T-shirt and hair piled in a bun on top of her head, she looked relaxed. Almost…content.

He'd keep that observation tucked away for now, though. Since their last conversation hadn't ended well, he didn't want to say or do anything to mess up the current situation. If she was happy here, he'd wait patiently for her to admit it. A declaration like that would have to be her own idea.

"Today was all right." She tucked a loose strand of hair behind her ear. "Thanks for the flowers."

"You're welcome." He couldn't stop a smile. "Did you like them?"

"They're nice." She lifted one shoulder. "I don't know much about flowers."

Huh. He tried to smother his disappointment. Didn't women usually love to receive flowers? Her pained expression hinted that she'd prefer to receive dental work. Or a bout of the stomach flu. Was she allergic?

He shifted carefully toward her, trying not to aggravate Adeline. The girl could pound a bottle of formula like nobody's business.

"We need to talk about Wade and Maggie's service." Kelsey's voice turned somber.

"Oh? Is there a date and time?"

"Mom sent me a text. Maggie's family and mine have agreed to August tenth."

"That's five days from now." He mentally calculated how he'd finish the harvest in time. It would be close, but he'd make it work. "I'll drive you."

"No, that's okay." She held up her palm. "Harvest is an intense season. I know how busy you are. Besides, I thought I'd go early and help out."

Was that really her intention, or was this a subtle attempt to take Adeline back to Wyoming? He hated that the ugly suspicion had seeped in. Hated that he'd assumed the worst. "It's not a big deal. We'll be finished and I can drive us."

Tension rolled in, thick and stifling like smoke from a raging wildfire.

"I don't need you to come home with me, Landon."
I don't need you, Landon.

Her rejection stung. Just when he thought he'd breached her walls of self-protection, she doubled down on her mission to keep him out. "Wade and Maggie were my friends, too. I wouldn't even think of missing their memorial service."

She rubbed her fingertips against her temple. "You don't have to miss their service."

"But you're going without me and taking Adeline."

"I'm driving separately, and yes, I thought she'd ride with me."

He bit the inside of his cheek to keep from popping off and sneaked a quick glance at Adeline. She'd drained the bottle then fallen asleep. Her head rested against his arm, and her little chest rose and fell. Her peaceful face reminded him that she was an innocent baby who needed love and protection, not two parents stuck in a constant cycle of squabbling.

Help me out here, Lord. I don't know what to say to make this right.

"I'm not saying you can't go," Kelsey insisted, pulling him back to the conversation. "Why are you getting so upset?"

"I'm not upset." Not yet, anyway. He set the bottle aside and slowly reached for Kelsey. Her skin was soft and warm as he covered her hand with his own. "I'm worried that once you get there, you'll find a reason to extend your visit, and since you have your car, then it will make sense—" He fought to keep the raw emotion from his voice. "To just stay."

Her mouth opened, then closed, then opened again. "I can't believe you'd accuse me of being so manipulative."

"And I can't believe you keep pushing me away. No

matter how hard I try to show you how much I care about you and our daughter, it's never enough."

I'm never enough.

Her eyes widened, then she pulled her hand away and jumped to her feet.

Landon winced as she crossed the room in long strides and stopped in front of the window, her arms wrapped around her torso. So maybe being vulnerable and transparent wasn't his best move.

"It's not easy for me to trust you. To trust anyone," she said softly, her voice wavering.

His breath hitched. He leaned forward a fraction, silently willing Adeline to stay asleep and longing for Kelsey to say more.

"I can't barrel into a packed arena on a dangerous animal and hope for the best." She slid her palms up and down her bare arms. "As much as I want to believe that you'll take good care of Adeline and be a wonderful father and trust you when you say that everything will be okay, the truth is I'm terrified to let you try."

The air left his lungs in a ragged whoosh, and he sagged against the cushions. He mentally scrolled through their interactions since Kelsey had showed up at his house. He'd followed Gage's advice. Shown up, kept his promises and never given her a single reason not to trust him. His friends and family had been more than generous.

But Kelsey still didn't trust him.

Adeline heaved a deep sigh, shifting in his arms. He froze, petrified that he'd disturbed her. That was all he needed.

"It's getting late." He scooted to the edge of the couch then stood. "I'll put Adeline down, and then I'll go."

He trudged down the hallway to Adeline's room. His legs felt like they weighed a thousand pounds each. When he settled her in her crib, she flung one arm over her head, her little fist clenched.

"Sleep well, baby girl." The night-light plugged in nearby cast a small golden circle of light into the room. He hovered at the rail, resisting the urge to reach in and smooth the back of his hand over her round cheek. His chest nearly split wide-open at the overwhelming love he felt for her already.

He'd do anything for her. Anything.

Except tonight's conversation had clobbered him. He had no idea what to do. Or what to say.

He turned away and walked back into the living room. Kelsey sat on the couch, hugging her knees to her chest.

"Landon—"

"Good night, Kelsey." He kept walking. "I'll text you tomorrow."

She didn't respond. He moved toward the door and let himself out quietly. So much for not wrecking an almost perfect evening. Staring up into the clear sky filled with a full, silver moon, he silently prayed for direction. He didn't want to lose Adeline. Or Kelsey. But hope was fading that they'd be able to find a way forward together.

Chapter Nine

Wow, she had not seen that coming.

One minute they'd been discussing the logistics for Wade and Maggie's service, and the next Landon had gotten very real. Vulnerable.

Her cheeks burned. Instead of being grateful, she'd tried to run, just like he said she did when things got hard. Worse, she'd dismissed everything he'd done for her and Adeline and called him untrustworthy.

Maybe the flowers had set her off. Such a romantic gift made her nervous. Or maybe his incredible ability to show up and look so good holding Adeline had prompted her comments. The reason didn't matter, really. There was no excuse for her behavior.

She owed him an apology. A grand gesture wouldn't hurt, either.

"Ba, ba, ba." Adeline squirmed in Kelsey's arms, clearly not interested in being held.

"I know, pumpkin. Let me pack this food and we'll go." Kelsey settled Adeline against her hip, then gathered the lunch she'd made for Landon.

Adeline fussed and leaned toward the bag of potato chips sitting on the kitchen counter.

"Hang on." Kelsey planted a quick kiss in Adeline's hair then moved her out of reach of the food. "This will only take a minute."

Adeline screeched and arched her back.

Kelsey gritted her teeth and rushed to the pantry to grab a brown paper bag. Adeline wasn't going to make this easy. Hopefully she'd be able to get to the farm, deliver lunch and her apology, then come back to the house in time for Adeline's afternoon nap.

While she'd learned to make a handful of decent meals, nothing in her measly repertoire was something she could cart out to the middle of a wheat field. Especially with a ten-month-old baby in tow. So she put a small container of fresh watermelon chunks in the bag and added a turkey and Swiss sandwich, then a half dozen brownies. If nothing else, the chocolate would be good. She added the chips last, tucked some napkins inside, then hurried toward the front door.

Adeline fussed all the way out to the car. When Kelsey opened the door to put her in her car seat, she realized she'd forgotten the diaper bag. Maybe she could go without it. Kelsey hesitated. Too risky. She left the food and went back for the bag. Adeline cried louder, twisting in Kelsey's arms and making it difficult to hurry.

"I get it. You're not a fan." Kelsey's stomach clenched in a hard knot. "I'm trying to do something nice for your dad, all right?" Maybe this was a terrible plan. She could find another time to apologize to Landon. This meal wasn't exactly impressive. He'd never know if she didn't deliver it. When she'd texted early this morning and asked if she could speak with him, he'd suggested meeting her during his lunch break and gave her directions. She'd come up with the bright idea to surprise him with lunch.

What if he teased her? Or Adeline cried the entire time and made meaningful conversation impossible?

She buckled Adeline in, offered a pacifier, then hopped in the driver's seat before she talked herself out of this. Terrible idea or not, she had to follow through, because she wouldn't be able to sleep tonight if she didn't at least try to apologize.

A green combine maneuvered through the field beside the dirt road. Dust hovered in the air over a truck carrying a load of wheat, the bright sunshine glinting off its mirrors. Kelsey fumbled for her sunglasses and slid them on.

A few minutes later, Kelsey pulled into a driveway in front of a modest one-level home. Landon had suggested meeting him under the carport beside the house. This farm belonged to a friend, apparently. She didn't ask for details. She'd been so nervous trying to figure out what to say that she hadn't stopped to think about whether they'd have an audience. She turned off the engine and got out of the car, stealing a glance at the carport.

Oh no. At least ten guys sat around long tables on folding chairs. The aroma of something delicious filled the air. She'd obviously interrupted a meal. Three women stood nearby, chatting. They all glanced her way when she closed her door and wiped her clammy palms on her denim shorts.

Landon stood and walked toward her, wiping a napkin across his mouth. Uncertainty flickered in his eyes.

She couldn't resist letting her gaze slide from the pale blue T-shirt to his faded jeans and worn leather boots.

"Hey." He stopped on the other side of her car. "Thanks for stopping by."

She twisted the key ring around and around her finger. "No problem."

The food she'd packed seemed like a lame contribution now. Especially since he'd already eaten. Adeline's muffled cries stopped her from offering an explanation. She opened the back door, leaned in and unbuckled her.

"Anything I can do to help?" Landon's voice was warm. Kind. He stopped beside her, holding the door while she settled Adeline in her arms.

Of course she'd stop crying the instant she spotted Landon. So aggravating.

"Hi there." Landon pressed his fingertip to Adeline's nose. She grinned and leaned toward him. "This is a sweet surprise."

"Yeah, I wanted to…" The weight of all those curious glances unnerved her. Adeline squealed with delight as Landon scooped her into his arms. He gently lifted her toward the sky, earning another exuberant squeal.

Oh, this was not going to be easy. Kelsey pinched the hem of her red T-shirt between her fingertips while Landon settled Adeline on his shoulders. She giggled and twisted her little hands in his hair. Huh. Funny thing. Her own fingers itched to do the same.

Warmth crawled up her neck, and she forced herself to look away.

"Did you stop by so Adeline could see me or…" Landon trailed off, his questioning gaze finding hers.

"I—I owe you an apology." She pushed the words

out quickly. "I'm sorry. Not just about last night, but the way I've responded to you since I've been here."

His eyes rounded.

Shifting from one leg to the other, she forced herself to continue before she lost her nerve. "You are trying your best with Adeline, and I get that. I'm sorry I've been so...hard on you. And I can see why you thought I was being manipulative about leaving for the memorial service without you."

"So I was right is what you're saying." His mouth twitched at the corners as he clasped Adeline's knees with his hands and bounced her gently up and down.

Kelsey pressed her lips together. Did she have to admit that part out loud?

His half smile made her insides dip and sway.

"It hurts to admit that, right?"

She nodded then quickly turned toward her car. "I brought you lunch."

"Ah, a peace offering."

Kelsey extracted the bag from the floorboards and handed it to him. "I didn't realize you'd have lunch here."

"Thank you." Landon carefully set the bag at his feet. "Four families work together to feed everyone a hot meal so if we have to work late into the night, we can."

"Oh." She ducked her head. "I didn't know."

"Hey." He stepped closer, his voice dropping low. Why did he smell that good after riding around in a combine? Like the outdoors and hard work. So unfair.

She tipped her chin up, determined to conceal her body's traitorous response to his approach.

"I appreciate the food. Don't worry, I'll eat it." He hesitated, those gorgeous hazel eyes still locked on hers.

"Is it safe to assume we'll be traveling to Wyoming together?"

She managed a nod.

"Good." Landon lifted Adeline from his shoulders, then kissed her cheek and handed her over to Kelsey. "I'm looking forward to it."

"Me, too." And she was. It would be nice to have someone along for the drive with Adeline. She wedged her sweet girl on her hip and stood there staring at Landon, unable to move. Instead of regretting her apology, she felt lighter. Relieved.

Landon opened his mouth to say something, but a man's voice bellowed across the yard.

"Let's go, Landon."

"I've got to head out." He smiled. "Thanks again for stopping by, and for bringing lunch. It's good to see you both."

"You, too," she managed to squeak out.

"There's a storm in the forecast, which means we'll have to hustle to finish up. If I don't come by for a few days, that's why."

"Okay." She bounced Adeline on her hip, partly to keep her from fussing but mainly to shake loose the disappointment settling in her abdomen. She'd wanted to limit her contact with him, and now she was unhappy that they wouldn't see each other.

Fickle girl. Stop it.

Landon inched even closer, his callused fingers clasping her forearm as he planted one more kiss on Adeline's forehead. Her pulse skyrocketed. He let his hand linger, and something undecipherable flashed in his eyes.

"I'll see ya." He winked then turned and strode away.

She watched him go, already missing that smile and wishing she didn't. And now she'd agreed to a road trip. She'd have to keep her attention focused on her family, because he couldn't know how he affected her.

The following Tuesday, Landon showed up on Kelsey's doorstep at 7:55 a.m. Five minutes early. He hoped his effort to honor her request to leave for Wyoming by eight might earn him some points. He'd undoubtedly need to cash those in later when his driving didn't meet her expectations or he said the wrong thing. He smiled, imagining her witty comments. This road trip might test his patience, but he was secretly thrilled they'd agreed to travel together.

While he dreaded Wade and Maggie's memorial service, he couldn't wait to see Adeline. Kelsey, too. The last five days had been grueling, and he'd fallen into bed each night at an hour far too late to visit the girls. While the harvest had produced an abundant supply of wheat, and he'd made enough to carve a dent in the debt he owed his parents and have some left over for Adeline, he hated that he'd missed almost a week of his baby girl's life. And ever since Kelsey had stopped by with lunch, his thoughts kept circling back to her. Circling back to the possibility of building a life together.

Lord, help me to trust that Your plans for me are good, he silently prayed, then knocked softly.

When Kelsey opened the door with her hair soaking wet, a frown on her face and a fussy Adeline in her arms, he tried for an optimistic smile. "Mornin'."

"I'm not ready." Her weary gaze slid toward Adeline. "We've had a rough start. Can you hold her, please?"

Without waiting for him to respond, she thrust Adeline into his arms. "Sure, not a problem." He chuckled at Adeline as she clutched a fistful of his T-shirt, and he drew a deep breath.

"Hi, pumpkin." He kissed her cheek, earning him an appreciative coo. At least one woman in this house was happy to see him. "Come on, let's play so your mom can finish packing."

"I am packed," Kelsey growled. "Well, almost."

Landon followed her inside and closed the door, determined to keep his comments to himself. Based on the plastic laundry basket sitting on the floor behind the paisley-print sofa with stacks of clean clothes inside, and the half-empty duffel bag slouched on the floor beside it, he mentally questioned her definition of "almost." Probably best not to say anything. They had a long drive ahead, and six hours in the car with a baby was probably going to require every single ounce of his patience.

He sank to the floor in the living room and set Adeline down beside him.

"Ba, ba, ba," she said, pushing onto all fours then crawling toward one of her baby toys.

"Hey, Kelsey. Check this out." Landon called for her while he reached for his phone.

Kelsey glanced up from behind the sofa where she stood, sorting the folded baby clothes into neat stacks. "Oh yeah. She's been doing that for a while."

"What?" He couldn't keep the irritation from his voice. "Since when?"

"I'm not sure." Kelsey shrugged, avoiding his gaze. "Two days ago, maybe?"

"Did you take pictures?"

"Sorry, I guess I forgot to send them."

Anger simmered in his gut, like hot magma, threatening to erupt. *Forgot?*

"I might have a short video clip on my phone. I'll send it to you later."

"Thanks." There was so much he wanted to say right now. Was she really that busy that she couldn't bother telling him about one of their daughter's major milestones? Did she think he didn't care?

The familiar sinister voices crept in, taunting him. *You'll never be a good enough father. You left her and now she'll never trust you.*

He drew a deep breath, fighting to keep his anger contained.

"Lord, I need You," he whispered quietly. Adeline glanced at him over his shoulder and gave him a slobbery smile. The tightness in his chest lessened some. It was hard to stay angry with Kelsey when Adeline grinned at him like that. She held up a toy, a clear tube with rainbow-colored beads inside that sounded like rain when she shook it. The same one Kelsey had brought to the park.

"Oh, nice," he said. "Is that your favorite?"

She instantly dropped it and picked up a stuffed monkey instead.

"A monkey. Always a good choice." Landon quickly snapped a picture then put his phone away. "What's your monkey's name?"

"Goo." Adeline thrust the monkey high in the air then screeched loudly.

"I've never met a monkey named Goo before. May I hold your monkey?" Adeline sat on her bottom and shoved the monkey in her mouth, staring at Landon while she gnawed on its arm. She was so stinkin' adorable he could hardly stand it.

"Kelsey, is there anything I can do to help?" He mentally calculated the six-hour drive to her parents' place, plus another hour or two of stops for diaper changes and lunch. He couldn't imagine Adeline tolerating a whole day in her car seat.

"Nope, I got it," Kelsey called over her shoulder as she hurried down the hall toward her bedroom. "Just keep an eye on Adeline."

Right. He sighed. Why did he think she'd let him help her?

A few minutes later, Kelsey returned with a container of wipes and two packages of diapers. "Did you bring that portable crib?"

He nodded. "I texted your mom. She borrowed a high chair and still has plenty of toys."

"What about the car seat? Are you sure it's installed properly?"

"I'm sure." He kept his voice even. "Feel free to double-check if you want."

"It's just that she doesn't ride in your car as often and you're not used to—"

"If you're concerned about my ability to drive, you are more than welcome to find your own ride to Wyoming. Adeline's coming with me, and I'm leaving in two minutes. You decide." He opened the door and stepped onto the porch. He'd had enough of her questions. And her doubt.

She trailed after him. "I didn't say you weren't a safe driver."

"You didn't have to." He kept walking. "Your expression said it all for you."

So much for the progress. After she'd visited and brought him lunch, he'd hoped their contentious conversations were a thing of the past. Now they had to spend the next several hours in a confined space, trying to keep a baby content.

He wasn't changing his mind, though. Not after he'd worked so hard to convince Kelsey they could make this trip together.

This would be the longest road trip of her entire life. Kelsey stopped in front of the silver midsize SUV parked outside. "Whose car is this?"

"My mom's." He opened the back door on the driver's side and carefully shifted Adeline to his other arm.

"What's wrong with your truck?"

"Nothing." He frowned over the roof of the vehicle. "You and Adeline will be more comfortable in this, that's all."

Oh. She opened the passenger door and dropped her purse inside, then circled around the back of the car to help Landon get Adeline buckled in her car seat.

He hesitated, Adeline squirming in his arms. His frigid gaze challenged Kelsey. "I've got this. You don't have to supervise."

"I'm not supervising."

His brows lifted.

Okay, maybe a little. She turned and walked away, pausing to survey the gear he'd loaded into the back of the vehicle. Oh, good. He had remembered the portable crib. And he'd brought extra diapers. How thoughtful. Maybe this wasn't going to be such a disaster after all.

"You know I've done this before, right?" Frustration

emanated from Landon like steam from a hot pizza. "I drove Adeline back from Wyoming without any help."

"Good." She slammed the hatch. "Then today should be a breeze."

Oh brother. This was not going well. She climbed in the front passenger seat, set her purse at her feet, then buckled her safety belt.

When Landon slid behind the wheel, she refused to look at him. So maybe she'd asked a few too many questions. That was her job, though. To make sure Adeline had everything she needed. Why did he get annoyed with her for being a good mother?

Adeline fussed, already expressing her frustration with being contained. Kelsey twisted to check on her, but the car seat was still rear-facing, and all Kelsey could see was her chubby little leg and her bare foot kicking the upholstered cushion. Landon gripped the steering wheel with both hands and stared straight ahead.

"Are you going to be able to handle this?" His voice was low and laced with impatience.

"Handle what?" She faced forward and heaved a sigh.

"Adeline crying for the next six to eight hours."

No. Kelsey bit back a groan and tightened her fists in her lap. She looked out her window so he couldn't see the panic probably etched all over her face. "She'll settle down."

Please, Lord, help her stop crying. Such a desperate prayer. She felt silly for even thinking it. Wasn't she supposed to be able to calm her own baby down? Allowing Landon to see her weakness only made her fight harder to conceal her worries. "Just go. It'll be fine."

Landon muttered something under his breath then turned the key in the ignition.

"Excuse me?"

"I said, 'Whatever you say.'"

"Good." Kelsey nodded, affirming his answer. At least his attitude had slightly improved.

Landon turned on the radio and scrolled to a classic rock station. Kelsey opened her mouth to object, then changed her mind. She'd tolerate his music preferences for now. There had to be at least some compromises, or they'd fight the whole way. She'd save her objections for more important issues, like his driving.

She sneaked a peek at him from the corner of her eye. Knowing Landon, he probably liked to drive well over the speed limit. The man used to love living life on the edge.

Forcing herself to pull in a deep breath, she stared out the window and mentally counted her blessings. Although she and Landon had gotten off to a rough start, at least she didn't have to make this drive alone. The weather was beautiful, and a cloudless blue sky promised a storm-free ride west.

Adeline's fussing soon escalated into screaming, and Kelsey's positive attitude crashed and burned. They'd barely made it to the interstate before Adeline's fit made Kelsey want to beg Landon to pull over and let her out of the car. But if they stopped every time she cried, they'd never get to Wyoming. Kelsey had promised her mom she'd be there in plenty of time to help get Maggie's family situated. She desperately wanted to keep that promise.

"Stop the car."

"What?" Landon tapped the brake. "Here?"

"Yes, here. We have to do something about her crying."

"Kelsey—"

"I'm serious, Landon. I can't stand to listen to her cry like that."

"All right, hold on." He slowed down, clicked on his blinker, then took the next exit ramp.

As soon as he pulled over in the gas station parking lot, Kelsey hopped out of the car then climbed in the back seat beside Adeline. Her little face was red, and tears dampened her cheeks.

"Oh, you poor thing." Kelsey smoothed the damp hair off Adeline's forehead. "You are really warm. We've got to get you out of here."

She quickly unbuckled Adeline, then pulled her onto her lap.

Landon shifted in the driver's seat and glanced at her. "Everything okay?"

"I don't know." Panic welled in her chest. "Why won't she stop crying?"

"Did you try her pacifier?"

Kelsey fished the pacifier from inside the car seat and offered it to Adeline, but she batted it away.

"Nope." Kelsey frowned. "Any other suggestions?"

"Is she hungry?"

"I just fed her breakfast."

"How about her diaper?"

"I changed her before we left." Kelsey couldn't keep the exasperation from her voice, especially since Adeline cried louder.

Landon scrubbed his palm across his face. "You asked me for suggestions."

"I know, but you're not helping."

She'd have to figure this out on her own. Kelsey lifted Adeline up and cradled her against her shoulder, but Adeline twisted away and tried to squirm out of her grasp. Was she reaching for Landon? Please, no.

"You can't ride up front," Kelsey said. "You have to go back in your car seat."

"She's never going to go for that, especially since you took her out."

"Oh, I didn't realize you were the expert on all things baby. Would you like to ride back here?"

"Sure." Landon shrugged one of his impossibly muscular shoulders. "If that's what it takes."

Kelsey pinched her lips together. *Really?*

She was supposed to be the one who nurtured and comforted Adeline, not him. The ugly feeling slithering through her abdomen made her feel worse. Great. Now her own baby's preferences made her jealous.

Get a grip, girl.

While it about killed her to admit Adeline preferred Landon, she couldn't stand listening to her cry, either.

"Fine. I'll drive." She climbed out of the car with Adeline in her arms and waited for Landon to trade places with her. Oh, she wanted to trust him. She really did. The hurtful words she'd spewed and all the times she'd dismissed his kindness weren't okay. She'd meant every word of her apology. Her confession about not being as fearless as him had also been genuine. Despite their progress in their relationship, the lingering doubts still clung to her, leeching her hope. He might be the fun dad who made road trips entertaining, but she worried that he wouldn't stick around for the long haul when life got hard.

And life was about to get hard, especially if she was thousands of miles away and he stayed here alone with their daughter.

Chapter Ten

T he midmorning sunlight streamed through the grove
of aspen trees flanking the cemetery. He'd rather take a
hoof to the sternum from the world's angriest Brahma
than say his final goodbye to Wade and Maggie.

This was awful.

He swallowed against the ache in his throat. Friends
and family lingered, even though the private service
had finished. He needed to leave before he completely
lost it. Reaching for Adeline's stroller, he leaned down
and peeked inside. She'd fallen asleep with her thumb
tucked in her mouth. Brown hair swooped across her
smooth forehead, and long lashes feathered her cheek.
Man, she'd been a trouper today. Not even a single
whimper or whine throughout the whole event.

Thank You, Lord.

He straightened and glanced around.

Kelsey's fingers sliding into the crook of his elbow
surprised him in the best possible way. She rested her
head against his shoulder. Warmth spread through his
chest. He leaned closer and pressed a tender kiss to
the top of Kelsey's head. Her shoulders shook as she

cried. Poor thing. Wade had meant the world to her. Maggie, too.

He let go of the stroller and pulled Kelsey into his arms. She buried her face in his white button-down shirt, wrapped her arms around his waist and sobbed.

Landon smoothed his hand over her long hair and held her close. "It's okay," he whispered. "I'm here."

Kelsey's entire body trembled. He boldly tucked her head under his chin. The animosity of yesterday's road trip had melted away. Maybe their shared grief would unite them. He'd prayed for another opportunity to show her how much he cared about her. How much he longed to put aside his past mistakes and start over. He completely understood her comments about being vulnerable and struggling to trust. It scared him to risk being vulnerable, too, but time was not on his side. Maybe grieving the loss of Wade and Maggie would be the final blow to that well-constructed wall she kept trying to build between them.

Her tears drew concerned glances from her mother standing nearby with her husband and Maggie's family. *She's okay*, he silently mouthed, desperately wanting to be the hero. Although stepping into that role was a dangerous choice. If he and Kelsey leaned on each other, they'd likely forge a stronger relationship, but she still had to honor her commitment to the navy. He couldn't ignore reality forever. She had to go back to Hawaii soon, and they'd be back to arguing over what was best for Adeline.

He wouldn't let that stop him from comforting her. No one expected her to be strong all the time. He'd hold her and carry her through, no matter what happened between them, because that was the right thing to do.

"I'm going to miss them so much." Kelsey pulled away and swiped at her tears with the back of her hand. "Wade's the only sibling I've ever had, and Maggie was like a sister to me."

"I know." Landon fished a tissue from his pocket and handed it to her. "He was my best friend. There's nobody else like Wade. Or Maggie."

Kelsey took the tissue and dabbed at the corners of her eyes. Her splotchy cheeks and red-rimmed eyes made his chest ache. "I'm here for you, Kelsey." He reached up and tucked a strand of her hair behind her ear. "Whatever you need."

She offered a wobbly smile. "Thank you."

"We should probably go soon. If there's anyone you'd like to speak to, I'll stay with Adeline."

"I'd like to say hello to Maggie's grandparents." Kelsey glanced up at him. Her coffee-colored eyes searched his face. "You don't mind?"

"Not at all. I'll wait right here."

She turned and worked her way across the green lawn toward an elderly couple holding hands, their expressions somber. Although he hated that they'd lost Wade and Maggie far too soon, he wouldn't trade this fragile peace he and Kelsey had established.

Adeline stirred, and Landon peeked inside the stroller. Thankfully, she stayed asleep. When he straightened, four of his and Wade's friends from the bull riding circuit walked toward him. They'd graciously served as pallbearers. Emotion tightened Landon's throat again, and he clenched his jaw to keep from falling apart.

"Thanks for being here." Landon choked out the words as he shook Morgan's hand. "I appreciate it."

Morgan clapped him on his shoulder, then looked away. He struggled to maintain his composure, too.

Holt was next, his black cowboy hat shielding his blue eyes. "Sorry for your loss. Wade was one of the best."

"He sure was. Thanks for coming, Holt."

Clay and Boone came next, their tanned faces pinched in agony as they shook Landon's hand and offered their condolences again. Then they stood in a circle, stomping at the ground with their boots while an uncomfortable silence descended.

Boone was the first to break the tension with a mischievous gleam in his dark eyes and a smile twitching at the corner of his mouth. "If you don't mind my asking, what's with the baby and the pretty girl crying on your shoulder?"

"Yeah, you've been holding out on us," Clay added. "Since when did you become a family man?"

Ouch. "Since I found out I was a dad."

"Wow, congratulations."

"No way," Boone said, a broad smile brightening his features. "That's great news."

"What's her name?" Holt peered inside the stroller.

"Adeline." Landon couldn't stop a proud smile. "And she's the best thing that's ever happened to me."

Normally such a bold statement in front of his friends would have earned him a fair amount of teasing. His friends would stop at nothing to give him a hard time for sounding so…love struck. This time, he didn't care. He was thankful for Adeline and the gift of being her father, even though he still had so much to learn.

"And the pretty lady?" Morgan nodded toward Kelsey. "Isn't she Wade's stepsister?"

Landon nodded. "We met at Wade and Maggie's wedding."

"Ah, yes. I remember. She was one of the bridesmaids. You two fell faster than Boone here getting bucked off a bull," Clay teased.

"Hilarious," Boone glowered. "Boy, you better not mess this up. Wade would tan your hide if he knew."

The laughter immediately faded. Boone's words stung, but Landon refused to let the comment get to him. He was done being angry about Wade keeping Kelsey's secrets, too.

"Wade knew about Kelsey and me. Adeline, too. That's why I'm not going to mess anything up."

He meant what he said. Although they had their differences and he'd definitely made more than his fair share of mistakes, from here on out he was going to do everything in his power to show Kelsey he could be the dad—and hopefully the husband—she needed and wanted.

Maybe she missed him.

There. She'd admitted the truth.

Except she couldn't have picked a worse time to conclude this, because Landon wasn't scheduled to spend any time with Adeline until tomorrow.

Stupid schedule. That had been one of her worst ideas ever, insisting that they stick to a regimented plan for coparenting. Besides, she didn't want to see Landon to work out a parenting plan or a visitation schedule or talk about Adeline's future. She wanted to see Landon because she couldn't stop thinking about him and it was about to drive her bananas.

She flopped on the couch while Adeline sat on the

living room floor, totally enthralled with the new toys they'd acquired in Wyoming. Maggie's grandparents, bless their hearts, had given her a wrapped present after the memorial service. Now the blue plastic piano was the only thing Adeline wanted to play with. Even though the repetitive sounds were jumping on Kelsey's last nerve, at least the thing kept Adeline occupied and she didn't have to chase her around the house, keeping her out of trouble.

Kelsey flung her arm over her eyes to block out the images of Landon that constantly invaded. Ever since he'd tenderly cared for her during Wade and Maggie's memorial service, held her while she cried, then looked after Adeline so she had time to help her mother care for her stepdad, her resistance toward him had ebbed. Then he'd let her sleep all the way back from Wyoming while he handled all the driving.

A man that selfless was hard to resist.

Except she was due back in Hawaii in less than a month. Leaving without him and Adeline made her want to weep. What a mess.

Someone knocked on her door, pulling her back to reality. She stood and crossed to the living room window. An unfamiliar car sat in the driveway. Not Landon. Bummer.

Skye and Laramie stood side by side on the porch. Kelsey opened the door. "Hey. What's up?"

"We're here to babysit so you can go to the Founder's Day festival." Skye grinned triumphantly. "Landon will be here in an hour to pick you up."

"I thought that was canceled." Kelsey leaned against the door frame and tried to ignore the way her pulse stuttered at the news that Landon was on his way.

"Rescheduled because of the hailstorm," Laramie said. "You were probably out of town when the decision was made."

"You might as well let us in, because we're not taking no for an answer," Skye added.

"Besides, you can't kick me out of my own house." Laramie smiled playfully, her hands splayed across her rounded abdomen. "Or deprive me of seeing my niece."

These two were something else. "When you put it like that, how can I possibly say no?" Kelsey smiled then stepped back and opened the door wider. "Come on in."

"Go get ready." Skye gently clasped Kelsey's shoulders and turned her toward the hallway. "We've got Adeline."

Clearly, arguing was a waste of time. She headed for her bedroom, mentally reviewing her clean clothes. Since she'd been an emotional wreck when she'd left Hawaii, her suitcase held an odd mix of shorts, T-shirts, a sweatshirt, one nicer outfit for church, a black dress, her favorite denim skirt and two pairs of jeans. Not exactly impressive. She hadn't been to a fall festival or a county fair or whatever tonight's event was all about in years. Did she have anything suitable?

She sorted through her limited options and chose her favorite jeans, a cream-colored tunic with a bold floral print and cowboy boots. The muffled sounds of Adeline squealing with happiness while Skye and Laramie played with her made Kelsey feel less nervous about leaving her baby. That left plenty of room for her insides to twist in knots about spending the evening with Landon. Sure, she'd missed him, but she didn't trust herself to be alone with him, either.

By the time she finished putting on her makeup and curling her hair, she heard his truck pulling up in front of the house. She applied some lipstick, gave her appearance one last glance in the mirror, then grabbed her purse and walked into the living room.

The front door clicked shut as Skye closed it behind Landon. When he saw Kelsey, his eyes widened, and a slow smile spread across his face.

"You look amazing."

Kelsey tightened the grip on her purse strap as butterflies took flight in her abdomen. "Thank you."

Skye and Laramie traded knowing glances. Before Kelsey could question their silent exchange, Adeline crawled toward Landon, her exuberant babble filling the room.

Landon chuckled, leaned down and picked her up, then thrust her in the air.

Adeline's bubbly giggle drew everyone's attention. With all eyes on her baby girl's wide-eyed smile, Kelsey seized the opportunity to let her eyes roam over Landon.

He wore a blue T-shirt the color of the Colorado sky, dark-wash jeans and brown cowboy boots. His blond hair was still damp and curled at the nape of his neck. The strong, tan arms supporting Adeline made Kelsey's limbs tremble. Now that he was here, now that they were about to be alone together, she mentally scrounged for reasons to back out. She'd gotten what she wanted— Landon here without delay—but was that really what she needed? Was *he* really what she needed?

Laramie held her phone, poised to take notes, and faced Kelsey. "Any specific instructions?"

The question pulled Kelsey from her thoughts.

"She drinks almost a full bottle of formula before

bed. If it's not warm, she'll refuse it and then she wakes up in the middle of the night—"

"Warm bottle of formula." Laramie's fingers flew over her screen. "Got it. What else?"

"She hates those sleep sacks, so I've been putting her to bed in her white pajamas with the yellow ducks. They're clean and hanging on the side of her crib." Kelsey paused. She didn't have too many nights left with her baby girl. Letting someone else put her to bed carved a hollow ache in her chest. "I try to read her one or two short books, and don't forget she still takes a pacifier. Oh, and the white noise—"

"Adeline will be all right." Landon shot her an empathetic glance. "They have kids, too, you know. They'll figure this out."

Heat climbed her neck. Why did he have to be so good at reading her emotions? "She asked for instructions."

Landon handed Adeline to Skye then turned and opened the door. "C'mon, let's go before all the funnel cakes are gone."

"Funnel cakes?" Kelsey rolled her eyes. "Really?"

"Obviously you've never eaten a funnel cake." Laramie ushered her toward Landon. "They don't last long around here."

"Good night, pumpkin." Kelsey hesitated as Adeline fussed. "I'll be back soon."

"She'll stop crying once we leave." Landon pressed his hand to the small of her back and gently guided her out the door.

"Call me if she doesn't," Kelsey called over her shoulder as she stepped out into the warm late-summer evening. This had better be the best festival with the most scrumptious funnel cakes of all time—otherwise she'd regret giving up a precious evening with Adeline.

A twinge of guilt pinched her insides. Okay, so maybe that was an excuse. If she was honest, her anxiety about being alone with Landon was the bigger issue. Somewhere between Wyoming and here, her feelings toward him had morphed from I-can-barely-stand-you to something that resembled I-can't-possibly-leave-you.

And this new reality frightened her. She couldn't afford to want him. Not now. Because wanting him meant talking about and planning for a future together. A future that had only ever revolved around her baby girl. She was terrified of allowing Landon into their lives permanently. If he messed up and let her down, she'd survive, but she couldn't imagine exposing Adeline to that kind of heartache.

He owed Skye and Laramie big-time.

A shovel-their-driveways-every-snowstorm and babysit-their-kids-six-weekends-in-a-row kind of debt. How they'd convinced Kelsey to let them watch Adeline for the night, he'd never know. But he was grateful.

Landon stifled a smile as he parked his truck in a crowded lot a block from Main Street in downtown Merritt's Crossing.

"Here we are." He cut the engine and hopped out. His heart wedged somewhere in the vicinity of his throat as he circled the truck and opened the door for Kelsey.

She climbed out, smoothed her hand over the front of her blouse and slid her purse strap over her shoulder. Her dark eyes surveyed the scene. "What's a Founder's Day festival, anyway?"

He gently closed the door behind her. His fingers

itched to reach for her hand, but he resisted the temptation and led the way across the gravel parking lot toward the sidewalk. "You said you were from Oklahoma, right? Didn't your hometown have an annual celebration?"

She fell in step beside him and fired an oh-please-you-can't-be-serious look his way. "I grew up in the city, cowboy, and I can't remember the last time I went to a county fair."

He grinned. Funny thing, her cowboy jab didn't get under his skin like last time. "You've been missing out."

"This is all just an excuse to eat funnel cakes, isn't it?"

"You got it." He waved to his neighbors standing in line to buy sodas. "It's also a great opportunity to dunk Mr. Weston in the dunk tank if you're so inclined."

"What did Mr. Weston ever do to you?"

Landon paused as a blonde teenage girl wound up and hurled a baseball toward the target. Mr. Weston yelled as his seat dropped out and he plunged into the metal feed trough full of water. Applause rang out while the girl thrust both hands in the air then high-fived her friends.

"He's the high school principal now, but when I was a student, he was a new teacher and a coach. He did not like me missing school on Fridays to travel to my bull riding events, so he threatened to fail me. There was also that one incident with the spray paint on the county water tower, but we don't need to go there."

"Sounds like there's more to that story."

"C'mon." He gestured toward the opposite end of the street. "Food's this way."

Pink and orange streaks coated the pale blue evening sky. Volunteers had blocked traffic from driving down Main Street, and the sidewalks were filled with tables displaying handmade crafts, treats for sale and simple carnival games with silly prizes. Kids laughed and chased each other, darting in and out of groups of adults chatting and laughing. The aromas of fried dough and sugar filled the air, mingling with the scent of hamburgers and hot dogs cooking on charcoal grills.

"You're not going to try to win me a stuffed teddy bear at the ring toss?" She stopped in the middle of the sidewalk and pointed to the table nearby. The gleam in her eye and her teasing smile gave him hope. Hope that she'd have fun tonight. Hope that she'd appreciate this slice of small-town life and want their daughter to grow up here.

"The ring toss and your teddy bear will have to wait." Landon kept working his way through the crowd. "I'm telling you, those funnel cakes won't last."

A few minutes later, they carried paper plates loaded with deep-fried golden cakes sprinkled with generous amounts of powdered sugar to an empty picnic table.

Landon settled on the wooden bench across from Kelsey and set a stack of napkins and two bottles of water between them.

Kelsey tore a small piece from her funnel cake then hesitantly took her first bite. He waited, watching for her reaction. When she stopped chewing, closed her eyes and released an appreciative groan, he thrust his fist in the air. "My work here is done."

She smiled, finished chewing, then quickly tore off a larger piece.

Landon chuckled and did the same. "Oh man. That's even better than I remembered."

"So good." Kelsey dusted the sugar from her finger-tips and reached for her water.

"Tell me again why you've never tried this?"

Her expression grew serious. "My dad was an addict. He and my mom divorced when I was in junior high, and they fought a lot because he wasn't very dependable. I was supposed to spend every other weekend with him and part of the summer, but he rarely showed up." She twisted the paper plate on the picnic table in a slow circle. When she raised her eyes to meet his, the pain lingering there made his heart hurt.

"I'm sorry," he said.

She looked away. "My mom didn't have time for fairs or festivals or much of anything fun. After my dad overdosed, we left the small town we'd been in and stayed with her cousin until she found a job. Sometimes she couldn't make rent, so we'd move in with a friend or her boyfriend. She tried to stick around the larger cities, because that's where she could find work."

Now it all made sense. The reason she'd kept their daughter a secret, why every time they took a step closer, she'd slam the door shut. She was afraid he'd repeat her father's mistakes. He reached across the table and took her hand. "And that's why you've worried about Adeline living with me."

She nodded slowly. Her eyes lifted to meet his. "I never want her to have to worry about whether her dad is going to be there for her. Whether he'd spend every cent he had to get his next fix. Whether her father will overdose."

"Kelsey." He breathed her name. "You don't have to worry. With God's help, I'm sober now."

Doubt flashed across her features. *Ouch.*

He caressed the back of her hand with his thumb. "I promise."

"I want to believe you."

"Even though I've given you plenty of reasons to worry, that's all in the past. I've learned from my mistakes, and I will be the most loyal and attentive father I can possibly be."

And the loving, dependable man you can trust with your heart. The words stuck in his throat. Too risky. Too vulnerable. Now that she'd revealed her doubts, the danger of scaring her off was far too great. He couldn't stand the thought of losing the two people he cared about most in the world.

The band set up on the makeshift stage nearby strummed the opening bars of a classic country song.

Landon stood and tugged Kelsey to her feet. "Let's dance."

"Oh, no, thank you." She shook her head. "The last time I danced with you, my entire life changed."

He couldn't stop a smile. His, too. But in a good way. Although he hadn't planned to start a family the way he did, that little girl meant the world to him. "One song. That's it."

Kelsey's beautiful eyes sparkled, but she stayed firmly rooted in place. "That's what you said the last time."

"You have my word this time. One song. Unless dancing with me is so amazing that you want to keep going, in which case I'm happy to oblige."

She heaved a dramatic sigh and let him pull her toward the other dancing couples. "You're impossible, you know that?"

"Impossible to resist."

Her melodic laughter fueled his confidence. Ignited another spark of hope. Now more than ever, he was determined to prove he was worthy of her love, because he couldn't imagine a future that didn't include her and Adeline.

Chapter Eleven

He'd done it again.

Landon had sweet-talked her into dancing. *Just one song.* Yeah, right. It was almost like he knew she couldn't resist him when he held her in his arms and guided her around the grocery store parking lot turned dance floor.

Someone had strung vintage bulbs between the trees planted in the center of the parking lot. Strands of clear lights decorated the temporary stage and arced over the band, casting a soft glow onto the musicians. At least a dozen other couples orbited around them. Kelsey recognized Skye's brother Drew smiling at a beautiful woman, the same one he'd been with at Pizza Etc.

She glanced up at Landon. His gaze locked on hers. The flecks of gold in his hazel eyes pulled her in, and she couldn't look away. The upbeat song perfect for two-stepping faded into a romantic ballad with a much slower tempo. Landon hesitated then stopped. He'd kept his word. They'd only danced one song. Her pulse sped. He held her hand in his while the other stayed respectfully on the small of her back.

She didn't want to stop dancing. One song wasn't enough. His eyes darkened, silently questioning her as she moved closer, savoring the warmth of his embrace. His gaze dropped to her lips. Her breath caught.

If she kissed him, they'd no longer be two people responsible for raising Adeline. If she was honest, she wanted him to be more than a guy she shared a child with. So much more. But letting him into her heart meant she'd have to abandon her claims and excuses that he was all wrong for her and admit that she'd made a mistake. Because if she kissed him now, she was deliberately choosing to step forward into the frightening unknown of a committed relationship.

Her thoughts went to battle with her emotions. This wasn't an innocent kiss at a fun small-town festival. The longing in his eyes hinted that she meant more to him than that. And if she didn't want him to kiss her, she needed to step away, because it wasn't right to string him along.

Landon's eyes ping-ponged between hers, then he moved closer. Their mouths were only a fraction of an inch apart now.

"Is this what you want?" he asked, his voice low and rough.

She barely nodded before his lips brushed against hers.

He tasted sweet, remnants of the sugar from the funnel cake still lingering. The tenderness in his touch and the way his palms moved to caress her face made her feel cherished. Wanted. When he slid his hands into her hair and deepened the kiss, the scent of his aftershave enveloping them almost made her forget what had happened the last time he'd kissed her like this. Almost made her forget the heartache of waking up alone.

She gave the doubts creeping in a desperate shove, then twined her fingers behind his neck and kissed him back. All her worries about his addiction and irresponsible behavior had faded away. He'd proved her wrong. Adeline adored him. He was the answer to her prayers and a solution to her family care plan problem. With Landon back in her life, she could return to Hawaii and do her job knowing Adeline was in his capable hands.

Until he messes up and lets you down.

The ugly truth barged in, wrecking their perfect moment.

She pressed her hands against his chest and firmly pushed him away. They stared at each other, heat smoldering in his eyes and her own chest heaving as she tried to catch her breath.

The band played on, and couples kept circling.

"Stop. We have to stop."

"Why?"

"You know why." She took a giant step back and planted her hands on her hips. "When you kiss me like that, it only gets us in trouble."

Hurt flashed in his eyes.

She turned and fled, stopping at the picnic table long enough to grab her purse, then hurried down the street.

"Kelsey, no. Don't leave!"

Landon called after her, but she refused to turn around, even though the desperation in his voice made her steps falter.

Fear pricked. She cut long strides down the sidewalk, sidestepping adults and children soaking up every single minute of the festival. She had to get out of here. That kiss had changed everything. Knocked her headlong into a scenario she'd hoped to avoid ever since she'd arrived. It had clouded her judgment and made her believe in a future that wasn't possible.

"Where are you going?" Landon's voice grew louder as he jogged up behind her. "We need to talk."

No, no more talking. He'd only try to convince her—again—that he was solid dad material. Relationship material. And even though she'd run out of sidewalk soon and end up back at his truck, just like last time, the adrenaline humming in her veins propelled her forward. Away from that dance floor and his kiss and the warmth of his touch.

The curious stares of onlookers heated her skin. She ducked her head and walked faster. Everyone in the county would probably be gossiping about them before the night was over.

Well, let them talk. She'd never planned to stay here long enough to care what anyone thought of her.

That's a lie. You do care, and you'd settle down here in a second if you could.

No. She tried to shake off the thoughts zinging through her head. Landon caught up, stepped in front of her and walked backward. She tried to go around him, but he shifted to his left, intentionally blocking her path.

"Talk to me." Concern etched his features. "What's wrong? What did I do?"

Sadness balled in her throat. Oh brother. *Really?* Now her emotions were going to betray her, too?

"Take me home." She forced the words out, then darted around him. "Please."

"Okay." He turned and faced forward, matching his steps to hers. Those amazing hazel eyes stayed riveted on the side of her face. Oh, why did he have to be so attentive?

Finally, they arrived at his truck. Instead of opening the passenger door, he leaned against it, blocking her from getting in.

"Move."

"Not until you explain why you're upset."

She pushed out a long breath. "Don't you get it? We're all wrong for each other."

"That kiss tells a much different story, sweetheart."

"The ending's still the same." Her words came out rough. Jagged. "You want to stay here and put down roots and grow wheat. I owe the navy another year, and then I'm going to nursing school."

"Ambitious plans." A muscle in his jaw flexed. "Where do Adeline and I fit in that bright future of yours?"

She swallowed hard. "We'll always have Adeline, but you and I don't have a future together."

He winced, then those gold-flecked eyes morphed into icy orbs. Laughter rang out somewhere behind them, and the band switched to a traditional song featuring a banjo solo.

Say something. She stared at him, willing him to break the tense silence.

"Well." He pushed away from the truck and straightened, his expression unreadable. "I guess you've got this all figured out then."

Wait. What? No argument. No cajoling. No snarky comeback. He was going to agree with her and give up without a fight?

"Since there's nothing left to say, I'll take you home." He stepped aside and pulled open her door.

"Everything okay?" Drew Tomlinson strode toward them, holding hands with the woman he'd been dancing with.

"Yes," Landon growled. "We were just leaving."

"No," Kelsey protested at the same time.

Drew's gaze toggled between them. "Why don't I give you a lift, Kelsey? Eden drove separately."

"You don't need to do that." Landon stood holding the passenger door open. "We're civilized adults, capable of riding in the same truck together for ten minutes."

Ha. Kelsey tipped her chin up. "I'm riding with Drew."

"Fine." Landon pushed the door closed. "Oh, by the way, Kelsey, I'm not giving up on Adeline. I'll be over at nine tomorrow morning to see her. Then we're making an appointment with an attorney and establishing a custody agreement. I'm not letting you take her to Hawaii. I'll file for primary parental responsibility if I have to."

"Fine."

She turned and followed Drew toward his truck. It wasn't fine. Not at all. But she climbed in and slammed the door, then waited while he walked Eden to her own car parked nearby.

Tears threatened to fall, and she dug her fingernails into her palms. Her lips still tingled from Landon's kiss, and the faint aroma of his cologne lingered on her clothes.

Primary parental responsibility. Would he really try to take Adeline from her?

Landon stood at the fence separating their field from their neighbor's, sipping coffee from his insulated mug and watching as Cal plowed the soil. The loamy scent of tilled earth filled his nostrils. Swallows chirped and soared overhead, while the morning sun streamed across the acres of land his family had tended for three generations. Harvesting and planting, testing the soil, assessing the seed, double-checking the nitrogen level in their fertilizer. He'd spend his days checking off all the tasks on their lengthy to-do list as they prepared to plant more wheat and try not to think about how nicely Kelsey had fit in his arms as he'd twirled her around the dance floor. Or how much his heart hurt when she looked him in the eye and insisted they had no future together.

The world kept turning, seasons changed, and somehow he had to figure out how to keep moving forward. Keep living, keep being productive, even after all his plans had derailed. He'd started over before, and he could do it again. Sighing, he checked the time on his phone. He and Cal had met early so they could get the plowing finished before the heat of the day set in. Although fall was allegedly just a few weeks away, the summer heat was still hanging on for dear life. While he had no desire to speak to Kelsey after what she'd said to him last night and then refused to ride with him, he wasn't reneging on his scheduled visit with Adeline.

"You guys got an early start." His father's voice stirred him from his thoughts. Landon turned and forced a carefree smile. Dad joined him at the fence carrying an almost identical insulated mug.

"Cal wanted to get going on the plowing. I just came by to make sure he had everything under control."

His father studied him. "Is plowing the only thing on your mind?"

Landon dipped his head and carved out a notch in the

dirt at his feet with his boot. "I'm going to have to hire an attorney. I'll file for primary parental responsibility if that's what it takes to keep Adeline in Colorado."

"I'm sorry to hear that, son," Dad said. "A tough situation for everyone involved."

"I know I still owe you and Mom more money, and I'm trying to provide for Adeline, too." He swallowed hard. "If I have to hire an attorney, I'll need to adjust my payments."

Man, he hated having this conversation with his dad. Hated that he still had a debt to pay off. He forced himself to look his father in his eyes. "I'm sorry."

Dad's green eyes filled with sympathy, and he clapped Landon on the shoulder. "You don't need to be sorry. You've carried a mountain of guilt and regret these last few years, I'm sure. We all make mistakes. Adeline has been a huge blessing in your life."

Landon nodded and looked away. He loved that little girl so much it hurt.

"Even though you and Kelsey have some differences to work out, as best as your mother and I can tell, you're both wonderful parents. Whatever we can do to support you, we're here, and we trust that you'll pay us back when you can."

Wow. He hadn't expected that. Not that his father had ever been harsh or punitive, but that gracious response made another wave of emotion crest inside him. He found his voice. "Thanks, Dad."

Cal turned the tractor around at the edge of the field and drove toward them. The hum of the engine got louder as he drove closer. Landon and his father both waved to the young guy through the windows on the side of the tractor's cab. As Cal continued across the field, Landon sensed his father's curious gaze.

"Can I ask you something?" Dad cradled his coffee mug in both hands.

Landon shrugged. "Sure."

"Have you been praying about what to do with Kelsey and Adeline and how to navigate life as a single father?"

"I've never prayed harder. And I've tried to do everything right, too. Gage told me I should keep my promises and do everything I can to show Kelsey that she can trust me, but—"

"But she's still afraid."

"Yep." Landon raked his fingers through his hair. "When she's afraid she runs, because that's what her mom did. Kelsey's dad was an addict who eventually overdosed, and she had a pretty lousy childhood."

"That's really sad."

"She's afraid Adeline's going to have the same tough childhood if she grows up with me."

His dad frowned. "But you have a solid family and good friends, a church community and so many people who love you and who will love Adeline, too. It's a shame Kelsey can't see that."

"That's why I need an attorney." Landon pulled out his phone and checked the time. "I've got to go. I said I'd be by to hang out with Adeline before her morning nap."

"You're doing the right thing." Dad smiled sadly. "Being an attentive father is hard work, but it's so rewarding. Adeline needs you to keep showing up for her."

"I know, I will."

"Your mother and I will keep praying."

"Thanks." Landon turned and walked along the fence until he got to his truck parked on the side of a dirt road.

He slid behind the wheel then drove toward Laramie's house. A ball of dread sat low in his stomach. While he was always happy to see Adeline, he wasn't ready to speak to Kelsey. Her words had wrecked him. Obliterated his hopes for the future. He'd done everything he could to win her heart, and still he'd failed.

Just like she'd said he would.

Another lap and another desperate attempt to outrun her anxious thoughts.

Still they hounded her. Taunted. Spurred her to run even faster.

Kelsey's leg muscles burned and her chest ached, but she forced herself to keep going. Sweat coated her skin, and her long braid thumped between her shoulder blades. She squinted into the bright sunlight, wishing for at least the third time that she hadn't forgotten her sunglasses back at the house.

She wasn't about to return unless she had to. Landon had stopped by at nine to see Adeline and spend the morning with her, so Kelsey wasn't due back at the house until noon.

The track behind the high school was empty, the perfect setup for pushing her body to the limit. She'd run until her legs turned into Jell-O. Until she didn't have a drop of energy left to devote to worrying about Landon.

Primary parental responsibility. Three words that terrified her. She'd looked it up online after Drew dropped her off last night. They meant exactly what she'd feared. Landon would petition the court or a social worker or somebody in a position of power to keep

Adeline here in Colorado while she went back to Hawaii. On paper it made perfect sense. The quick fix to her caregiving dilemma. No doubt her commanding officer would sign off immediately.

Child safe and cared for by a biological parent? Check.

Trustworthy grandparents and extended family close by for backup? Yes and yes.

Enlisted navy diver ready and able for duty? Check.

But a satisfactory care plan and a legal agreement did nothing to ease her worries. Landon couldn't possibly be responsible for a baby who'd soon become a busy toddler.

Her running shoes pounded the rubbery surface, and her knees ached as she rounded the turn on the track's inside lane. Her mind pinged back and forth between memories of that kiss and how much she'd enjoyed the safety and security of Landon's arms holding her, and Adeline sitting alone on the living room floor, crying. The first image teased her with some mirage of happily-ever-after. A complete family, including a man who wouldn't leave her or her daughter.

Nonsense. Of course he'd leave. Or at the very least, mess up and let her down. To imagine anything different was to conjure the stuff of fairy tales and picture books. She refused to allow such silly notions to cloud her thinking. Broken promises, lonely weekends, humiliating school functions where she'd always cried, convinced she was the only girl there without a dad.

That was the reality she'd endured.

She pumped her arms, demanding that her body go faster, run harder, striving desperately to shove those terrible thoughts out of her mind. She wanted to see the good in Landon. To believe that all his interactions with Adeline pointed toward a wonderful, loving relationship. More than anything, she wanted to put her fears to rest and trust that he'd always show up. For her and for Adeline.

Stubborn, stubborn girl. What if you're wrong about him?

The thought blindsided her, promptly shortening her stride. She slowed from sprinting to a jog, blood pounding in her ears. She wasn't wrong. Was she? What some might call stubborn, she'd consider savvy. Street smart. A wounded little girl who'd become a proactive single mother. Sure, she'd read a few verses in her Bible about how she wasn't supposed to be afraid. She'd even cracked open the journal thing Skye had given her and read a section about how she was supposed to tell the Lord all her fears. She'd tried praying about finding a guardian for Adeline. Nothing had happened.

What did a lack of clarity even mean? Was she supposed to keep waiting and pray harder? Except part of her couldn't outrun the notion that maybe Landon was the right person to care for Adeline. The more time that passed, the more that thought latched on, and she couldn't shake it loose. He'd sneaked past her defenses. His smile, thoughtful gestures and tender care of Adeline had catapulted him across the moat she'd built around her heart. He'd almost won her over.

Almost.

Except loving him was too hard. Too frightening. She couldn't let him have sole responsibility for Adeline—or stake a claim on her heart.

Chapter Twelve

The text alert pulled Landon from a deep sleep. *Stop. Make it stop.*

He pushed off the blankets, groaning as he fumbled in the darkness for his phone. Scrubbing the sleep from his eyes, he clutched the device and squinted at the screen.

A fire call at the silos.

Please, God. No. A fire at the silos was one of their worst fears. Adrenaline pushed him out of bed, and he stood and hurried to his closet. His mind raced with ominous thoughts as he pulled on a T-shirt, jeans, a plaid button-down and socks. After a productive harvest, the silos were packed with grain. A fire would decimate not only the structure but the farmers' profits, too.

Fear roiled in his gut, propelling him down the hall. He stopped by the front door, shoved his feet into his boots, then grabbed his wallet and keys and jogged toward his truck. He'd forgotten his phone on his nightstand, but there wasn't time to turn back. Every second was crucial.

He made sure his gear was in the truck, then started

the engine and backed out of his driveway. His headlights shone in the darkness when he turned onto the road, reflecting in the eyes of a deer darting across his path. He tapped the brakes. The animal leaped the fence then vanished into his neighbor's field.

His heart hammered as he sped up, racing down the road. The clock on the stereo read 4:17, and a thumbnail of a moon hung in the night sky.

Landon made it to the co-op in record time. An ominous orange glow crowned the silos as flames licked the edges of the four containers.

He parked and hopped out, then pulled on his fireproof pants, jacket, gloves and helmet.

"We need water over here!" the volunteer chief yelled, directing the lone fire engine to pull closer.

Landon hurried toward the silos, joined by Drew and two other guys who'd already pulled on their gear. "Anyone in the containers?"

"Don't know." Drew's jaw tightened. Landon's stomach plummeted to his toes and propelled him into action. They had to find out. Even though it was the middle of the night and climbing inside the containers was dangerous to do alone, it wasn't wise to assume no one was in there. Trains and trucks passing through in the early morning hours, ready to transport grain and corn, might've required someone on-site to monitor the process. Sometimes that meant a person had to work inside the silos shoveling the grain.

While the rest of the volunteer firefighters directed the hoses and water toward the flames, Landon surveyed the scene. Acrid smoke stung his nostrils. The heat from the fire made him sweat.

He turned and studied the old house next to the

silos—nothing more than a modest one-room shelter, really. Probably left over from the days when the owner paid somebody to live there and maintain the silos.

"The fire's spreading!"

The ominous words sent a tingle coursing down his spine. Flames had engulfed most of the silos and moved on to eating up the dry grass beside the shack. They were running out of time to find and rescue anyone who might be trapped.

Landon moved closer to the shack. His chest tightened as he spotted a motionless form lying on the ground.

"Over here." He motioned for Drew and the others to follow. He hurried, although the ache in his back hindered his speed. When he got to the person's side, he noted the man looked young, maybe early twenties. Landon dropped the splint bag and the automatic external defibrillator he'd grabbed from the truck in the dirt then sank to his knees.

"We shouldn't move him," Drew said, hovering beside Landon.

"He can't stay right here," Landon argued. "The fire's getting closer."

"But what if he has a neck injury?"

Landon pressed his fingertips to the man's neck. "No pulse."

One of the volunteer firefighters sank to his knees opposite Landon and put his ear close to the man's face. "He's not breathing."

"We have to move him." Landon gestured for Drew to lift the man's shoulders. "I'll get his legs."

"Landon—"

"Drew, we either risk a neck injury and move him

to a safer location, or he stays right here and we all get hurt when the flames get too close."

"All right," Drew agreed. "Let's go. On three."

"One, two, three," Landon grunted, lifting the man's legs. The other guys moved in, supporting the tall, muscular man's frame. Landon's back protested, but he pushed through the pain, determined to do everything he could to save a life.

When they'd moved a safe distance from the shack and the fire, they lowered him to the ground.

"I'll start CPR," Drew said. "Landon, we need the AED."

While Drew started chest compressions, Landon quickly retrieved the unit, then opened the case. One of the other volunteers had shears in his pocket and cut the guy's filthy T-shirt off. Landon applied the pads to his chest, then waited for the machine to assess his heart rhythm.

Once prompted to stand clear and apply a shock, they slid back a safe distance then Landon pressed the button. His hands trembled as they waited for the computer to analyze the man's heart rhythm again.

Please, Lord. Help. Don't let us lose him.

"Still nothing." Drew frowned, then obeyed the prompt to resume CPR.

Finally, the man coughed and sputtered, then his eyes fluttered open.

Landon heaved a sigh of relief. He wanted to weep.

Sirens wailed as the ambulance pulled up, blue and red flashing lights adding to the chaos. Landon stole a glance over his shoulder. The fire wasn't out, but the volunteers had managed to contain it.

He stood and moved out of the way as the paramedics approached. Drew gave them the information they needed. A few minutes later, they had loaded the man into a waiting ambulance.

Exhausted, Landon made his way to his truck. Shedding his gear into the truck bed, he took the sports drink Drew offered him.

"Thanks," he whispered, his throat raw. He twisted off the cap and forced himself to take a sip.

"That's the worst fire I've ever seen." Drew gasped, his chest heaving as he dropped his firefighting gear then mopped the sweat from his forehead.

Landon nodded. Grain dust, oxygen and a confined space were the perfect ingredients for a fire. All it needed was a spark from a piece of equipment.

The owner of the silos stood a few feet away, talking to the sheriff.

His body still pouring sweat, Landon gritted his teeth and forced in a few deep, calming breaths. Adrenaline hummed in his veins. He was hot and tired and smelled terrible, yet his body still trembled from what he'd experienced.

When the equipment was stowed and the chief dismissed all the volunteers, Landon climbed into his truck and drove home. While they'd saved a life, the silos and their contents were a total loss. He had no way of knowing if they'd lost any wheat from their farm. He clung to the hope that it had already been transported to mills or ports out west. They'd find out soon enough. Just thinking about a devastating financial hit twisted his insides.

The intensity of the fire, Kelsey's rejection and the dreaded meeting with an attorney scheduled a few hours from now combined to send him into an emotional tailspin. By the time he parked in front of his house, a terrifying, hopeless feeling had taken him captive.

The pills in the glove box. You know you want them.

He white-knuckled the steering wheel and willed himself to be strong. For Adeline. He had to fight his way through this.

You're weak. A coward who can't handle pain. Once an addict, always an addict.

The harsh accusations rained down, chased by the smooth, tantalizing lies that had always, always led him astray.

Go ahead. You deserve to feel good.

He didn't have the strength to fight anymore. Leaning across the center console, he opened the glove box and knocked the truck's user manual, a flashlight and a box of bandages to the floorboards. A desperate longing surged through his body. Finally, his fingers grasped the plastic bottle.

"Oh, thank you." He popped open the lid, tapped the edge against his hand until three white tablets landed in his palm. His body responded, aching for respite from the pain.

He hesitated, staring at the pills.

This is the last time. No one will find out.

He squeezed his eyes shut, desperate to silence the lies. Because it wouldn't be the last time. If he took these pills, he'd slide into an abyss he wasn't sure he'd ever climb out of. Worse, he'd destroy any hope of a future with Kelsey and Adeline.

He opened his eyes and stared at his palm again. The pills taunted him. Toyed with his mind. Reminded him how quickly the razor-sharp pain would soften. How he'd relish the feeling of floating.

He left his gear in the back of the truck, tossed the empty plastic bottle in the dirt and stumbled into the house. Inside the door, he strode to the bathroom, dropped the pills in the toilet, then flushed them.

There. His head throbbed, and his heart pounded. He sucked in a ragged breath. Dark spots filled his vision as he sank to his knees and went facedown on the hardwood.

Adeline. Kelsey. They were the last people he thought of before his world went dark.

Kelsey checked the time again. Nine thirty-four. Pacing between the living room and kitchen, she stopped and looked out the window. No sign of Landon's truck coming down the road. He hadn't texted or called, either. He was officially thirty-four minutes late. Not that she was in a hurry to get to their appointment with the attorney in Limon. She'd rather go through boot camp again than face Landon and this attorney, but she didn't have another option. There wasn't anyone else to take care of Adeline, and she and Landon weren't going to establish a plan without mediation.

She sighed and glanced out the window again. Nothing. "Come on, Landon. Where are you?"

They had to drop Adeline off at Jack and Laramie's place first. If they didn't leave soon, they'd be late.

Adeline crawled across the kitchen, her little hands and knees slapping against the floor as she babbled, "Ma, ma, ma." It was sweet, really. And Kelsey would probably stop and take another quick picture if she weren't so worried.

Landon hadn't missed a scheduled visit or gone back on his word the whole time she'd been in Merritt's

Crossing. Even though she'd doubted and accused him and assumed he'd mess up eventually, part of her had hoped he wouldn't.

She found her phone and called him again. Straight to voice mail. Texting him was useless, too, because he hadn't responded to the two messages she'd already sent.

What if something had happened?

She quickly brushed the thought aside. He'd probably forgotten. Or overslept. What if he'd changed his mind and hadn't called to tell her the appointment was canceled?

Not likely.

She sent Laramie a quick text to let her know she was running late because Landon hadn't come by yet. Then she tucked her phone in the side pocket of the diaper bag and headed for the door.

"Come on, cutie pie." She stopped in the entryway and intervened before Adeline put a shoe in her mouth. "Let's go find your dad."

Adeline protested as Kelsey picked her up, dropped the sneaker by the door and hurried outside.

After putting Adeline in her car seat, Kelsey stashed the diaper bag on the floor then closed the door and climbed behind the wheel. She tuned the radio to a popular country station and tried to focus on the morning show hosts' entertaining banter while she drove toward Landon's house. Anything to keep her mind from imagining worst-case scenarios. A flawless blue sky surrounded her, and she had to squint at the bright sunshine streaming into the car.

A few minutes later, she pulled into his driveway.

The sight of his truck parked in front of the farmhouse sent anger sluicing through her veins.

"I knew it." She pounded her fist against the steering wheel, then parked behind his truck and hopped out. He'd stood her up. She opened the back door, grabbed her bag from the floorboards, then unbuckled Adeline from her car seat.

"Come on, sweetie. Let's go have a little chat with your dad."

"Da, da, da." Adeline offered a toothy grin as Kelsey settled her on her hip.

What was so important that he couldn't take the time to call or text and let her know he was running late? She strode toward the house. An empty pill bottle lying on the ground beside his truck caught her attention. She halted her steps. Her heart whacked against her chest wall as she stared at the container.

Oh no. Please, no. She nudged it with her toe, just enough to read Landon's name and the name of the pain medication on the label. Hydrocodone. She raced toward the farmhouse as quickly as she could with Adeline bouncing in her arms. The sweet baby girl's giggle floated into the air.

Kelsey pounded on the door. "Landon, open up."

She waited a split second, then rattled the doorknob. It twisted in her hand. She pushed the door open and hurried inside, nearly tripping over his body facedown on the hardwood floor.

No. She set Adeline on the floor and dropped to her knees beside him.

"Da, da, da." Adeline patted Landon's shoulder with her tiny palm.

Hot tears burned the backs of Kelsey's eyes as she shook him. "Landon, wake up."

He didn't move.

Her fingers trembled as she reached out and located his pulse on his neck. It was weak. His skin felt cool and clammy. She leaned closer and noted his shallow breathing. "Thank You, Lord."

Pushing to her feet, she fished her phone from her bag. She had to get help. Tears blurred her vision as she called 911.

"Landon, why did you do this?" She wished that the empty bottle in the driveway meant nothing, but she was certain that couldn't be the case. It had to mean something awful. Her worst fears confirmed.

"Nine-one-one, what's your emergency?"

"Possible drug overdose. Please, send help." Kelsey's voice broke. "I don't know how long he's been like this."

Adeline sat on her bottom beside Landon's head and jammed her thumb in her mouth, her blue eyes locked on Kelsey. Oh, she hated that her baby girl had to see this. Even if she was too young to remember, the sirens and paramedics were going to scare her.

"Tell me exactly what happened," the woman on the phone instructed.

"I—I'm not sure." Kelsey pressed her palm to her forehead. "I found him like this. Passed out on the floor, and there's an empty pill bottle in the driveway."

"Is the victim conscious?"

"No."

"Breathing?"

"Yes, and he has a faint pulse."

"Good. Do you know the victim's age?"

"Um, I'm not sure. Thirty-two?"

"Name and address?"

"Landon Chambers, and the address…" Blood pounded in her ears. She paced the floor, searching for a magazine or a bill or anything with an address printed on it. "I—I don't know. The big farmhouse next to the—"

"If you don't know the address, I'll find it. Are you alone with the victim?"

"No, my—our—baby is here."

"I want you to stay on the line until the ambulance arrives. Can you do that?"

"Yes, absolutely."

Every inch of her wanted to pick Adeline up and flee, but she couldn't abandon Landon. Not now. Not until help arrived.

She rubbed her palm against the tightness in her chest. "What should I do while I'm waiting?"

"Is he lying on his back or his stomach?"

"Stomach."

"If he vomits or has a seizure, is he lying in an area that's safe?"

The dispatcher's question provoked a fresh wave of fear.

"I—I guess." Kelsey surveyed the scene. "He's on the floor inside his house."

"If you're able, roll him onto his side, because it prevents aspiration of fluid should he vomit. If you can't, then it's best to leave him be. Unless you are concerned a bookshelf or a table or anything close by might fall on him. Also, make sure you and the infant are safe."

"Okay, I'll try to prop him on his side." Kelsey switched the call to speakerphone and set it on the floor, then dropped to her knees beside Landon again. She clutched his shoulder and torso with both hands and tugged, but it was no use. He didn't budge.

She picked Adeline up and held her close. "I can't move him. My daughter and I are safe, though."

"That's okay. Help is on the way. Stay on the line. You're doing the right thing." The dispatcher's gentle encouragement made Kelsey's throat ache. The whole situation felt surreal. *Why did you do this to me, Landon?*

A few minutes later, wailing sirens filled the air outside, and Adeline's eyes widened as she twisted in Kelsey's arms to see where the noise was coming from. In her rush to get into the house, she'd left the door open. She grabbed her phone.

"The ambulance is here."

"Excellent. Don't hang up yet."

Hurrying to the porch, she waved to the ambulance driver, who stopped behind Kelsey and Landon's vehicles. Although the driver turned off the siren, the red and blue flashing lights kept blinking in the morning sunshine. Two uniformed paramedics climbed out and hurried toward her.

"Kelsey?" The first, an older man with black sunglasses pushed up on his close-cropped dark hair, led the way.

"Yes." She stepped aside as his boots clomped up the steps. "Landon Chambers is the victim. He's on the floor inside. I'm certain he took too much hydrocodone. The empty bottle is still on the ground beside his truck." She was babbling, but she didn't care. Wasn't she supposed to tell them everything she knew?

The second paramedic, a woman about Kelsey's age, with her strawberry blond hair secured in a neat ponytail, paused and gently squeezed Kelsey's arm. "Thank you for the information. We'll take it from here."

"You're in good hands," the dispatcher said.

"Thank you," Kelsey whispered and ended the call.

Adeline started to cry, and Kelsey struggled to swallow back her own tears. She went down the steps and paced the yard, forcing herself to draw in deep breaths. Adeline kept crying, her little finger stuffed in the side of her mouth while she twisted in Kelsey's arms to stare at the ambulance.

Fragments of conversation filtered toward her, and their radios chattered with more details from the dispatcher, but Kelsey couldn't make sense of any of it. *Please, Lord. Save him. For Adeline's sake.*

A few minutes later, the stretcher carrying Landon disappeared into the back of the ambulance, then the medics closed the doors. Adeline cried, pointing as the vehicle pulled away from the house.

"I know." Kelsey kissed her damp cheek while hot tears burned the backs of her eyes. Landon's poor choices had wrecked her. Now that she knew he was safe, she wouldn't waste another minute in this town.

Her worst fears had come true. He'd betrayed her and Adeline. Leaving was the only option.

Chapter Thirteen

Kelsey. Adeline. He had to get to them.

Forcing his eyes open, he squinted against the bright light bursting through the vertical blinds.

"Hi, sweetheart."

Landon slowly turned his head toward his mother's soothing voice. She sat in a blue vinyl recliner beside his bed. The familiar beep of a machine nearby, boring white paint on the wall behind her and the lingering scent of astringent in the air confirmed his fear.

He was in the hospital. What had happened? Fragmented images replayed in his mind. A fire. The heat making him sweat. Working with Drew to help the guy whose heart had stopped.

The pills. Regaining consciousness in the back of the ambulance.

Oh no. He opened his eyes and slowly surveyed the room. No one else was with them.

"Where's Kelsey and Adeline?"

His mother's hopeful expression melted.

No. He squeezed his eyes shut, then opened them

again. His throat was raw and scratchy. "They left, didn't they?"

"Let's focus on making sure you're well."

Why wouldn't she give him a straight answer? He grunted and pushed up on his elbow, then flung the white sheet aside. "How long ago?"

"Whoa." Mom stood and grasped his shoulder, gently restraining him. "You need to rest. The doctor hasn't discharged you. Besides, you still have an IV."

Landon glared at the tube feeding a clear liquid into his vein. "I'll rest later. I need to stop Kelsey before she leaves town."

His mother's hesitation confirmed his fear. The truth slammed into him. He dragged his gaze to meet hers. "I'm too late, aren't I?"

She nodded. "She's gone, sweetie."

"Where?"

"She didn't say. I imagine back to her folks' place in Wyoming."

"No." He pushed his hand through his hair, hating the IV that tethered him to the bed. "She can't. We had a deal."

"I haven't spoken to her. Laramie texted her, but Kelsey hasn't responded. She probably feels your agreement is off since you—"

"Since I what?"

"She found the empty pill bottle on the ground." Mom rubbed his upper arm. "The paramedics told the doctor in the ER that you'd taken the hydrocodone."

"But I didn't." Blood roared in his ears. "I flushed them. Inside."

"Oh, thank You, Lord." Mom pressed her palm to

her chest and slumped back in the chair. Tears welled in her eyes. "I'm so glad to hear that."

He swung his legs over the side of the bed. "I have to fix this."

"I can try to call her."

"No, I need to get out of here first." He glanced around the room. "Where's the nurse or the doctor, or whoever has to sign the paperwork to discharge me?"

His entire body felt like someone had beaten him with a baseball bat, but he wasn't about to let that stop him. Yeah, he'd almost messed up and taken those pills, but with the Lord's strength he'd made the right choice. Now he had to make things right with Kelsey. Starting with driving to Wyoming to find her and Adeline.

"Honey, I'm not sure leaving town is a wise decision. Why don't you give it a couple days? If you're not still dehydrated, I'm sure they'll send you home soon. Once you're fully recovered, then maybe have a sensible phone conversation with Kelsey."

"Sensible isn't an option." He pressed his forehead into his palm. "She's furious. I guarantee it."

Honestly, she had every right to be angry. He was aggravated with himself for being so weak and keeping those pills in the truck. And why didn't he trash the bottle, too? That was why he had to get to Kelsey before it was too late. He'd apologize, beg for her forgiveness, commit to attending counseling and more therapy. If she wanted him to move to Hawaii, he'd consider that, too. Whatever it took to keep them both in his life.

"What if she left with Adeline already? Or made arrangements to enroll her in a daycare in Hawaii or hired some stranger to babysit her all the time?"

He stopped talking. The panic invaded, making his

pulse race. He had to talk to her. While he didn't blame her for being upset with him and fully acknowledged that he had let her down, some small part of him wondered if she knew he'd saved a guy's life. No, that didn't justify almost taking the pills, but selfishly he hoped she knew the truth.

"I know you're hurting and the thought of not seeing your daughter makes you upset, but you're not in any shape for a road trip."

He found a remote on a cord buried underneath his bedsheet. A red button in the center displayed a phone icon, and he pressed it. There. Maybe that would get somebody's attention.

"I appreciate your concern, Mom, but I don't have time to sit around weighing the pros and cons. Kelsey could be packed up and on her way to the airport with a one-way ticket to Honolulu by now."

He had to stop her.

The door opened, and a woman stepped in. Her sneakers squeaked on the linoleum as she grabbed the cart by the door with the computer and wheeled it to his bedside.

"Mr. Chambers, I'm happy to see you're awake." Her brown eyes crinkled at the corners when she smiled, and she wore her salt-and-pepper hair in a short, spiky style. "How are you feeling?"

"Good. Great, actually. No pain at all." He lifted his arm. "Can you pull this thing out? I've got to go."

She reached into her black scrubs and retrieved her stethoscope. "I need to check your vitals, then we'll talk about next steps."

"My vitals are super." He offered his most charming

smile. "If you'll get the doctor to sign off on my paper-work, I'll be all set."

"Let's make sure your lungs are clear."

He stifled an impatient groan. What did his lungs have to do with dehydration and saving a guy from a fire? His breathing sounded fine.

She stood beside him and pressed the stethoscope to his back. "Take a deep breath for me."

He obeyed.

"One more."

He sat up straighter and filled his lungs.

"Good."

She glanced at the numbers on the monitor beside him, then returned to the computer.

"What do you think? Everything good to go?"

She ignored his questions, her manicured fingernails clacking over the keyboard as she entered mysterious data. He tapped his hand against his thigh, mentally cal-culating how long it would take him to grab a change of clothes and a few essentials from the house. If he hustled, he might make it to Kelsey's parents' place before dark.

The longer he had to sit here, the more his stom-ach filled with a desperate, hollow ache. He wanted to drink about a gallon of water because his mouth was so dry, but he refused to admit any of that. Otherwise she might try to keep him here longer.

"Any pain?"

"Nope." He knew the drill from his bull riding days. He'd keep telling her no until she stopped asking.

She eyed him skeptically. "No pain at all?"

"None." He gestured to the IV in his arm again.

"Now can you pull this out? Please? Like I said, I really need to get going."

"Landon."

He bristled against the doubtful tone in his mother's voice. Wasn't she supposed to be on his side?

"You can't drive to Wyoming alone."

He glanced over his shoulder and shot her an impatient look. "We just talked about this. I need to get to Kelsey before she tries to take Adeline to Hawaii."

The nurse's curious gaze pinged between them. He half expected her to add her own commentary, backing up his mother's opinion. Instead, she put her stethoscope away and rolled the computer on its cart back toward the wall. "The doctor is with a patient in the next room. She'll be in shortly."

Shortly. That didn't inspire confidence. This time he didn't bother to conceal his frustration. He groaned and stared at the ceiling. Defeated. At this rate, Kelsey and Adeline would be in an airplane somewhere over the Pacific Ocean before they discharged him.

All he wanted was to see Kelsey face-to-face, apologize for making her believe the worst had happened and tell her that he loved her and couldn't imagine life without her. A simple plan, really. And one that was becoming next to impossible to execute.

The next morning, Kelsey sat on her mother's porch, exhausted and numb. No matter how hard she tried to avoid thinking about Landon, the image of his body on that stretcher going into the ambulance kept replaying in her mind.

Shivering, she pulled the orange-and-yellow-checkered quilt tighter around her shoulders. In the distance, cattle grazed in the fields against a backdrop of majestic mountains. The wooden rocker creaked as she glided back and forth, holding an insulated mug filled with coffee between her hands. Birds chirped, and a chill filled the air, hinting at autumn's arrival.

She blinked against the grit in her eyes left behind from a night spent crying then tossing and turning in her mom and stepdad's guest room. She'd finally given up and crawled out of bed just after 6:00 a.m. Adeline was still sleeping in the portable crib, so she'd crept outside on the porch with her coffee for a few minutes of peace. While she'd planned on praying, the words wouldn't come.

Leaving Merritt's Crossing with Adeline had been the right decision, hadn't it?

It was her only option, really. At least that was what she kept telling herself as Colorado disappeared in her rearview mirror yesterday. He'd started using again, and she couldn't allow their daughter to live in that kind of environment. Still, she wanted to believe that this was all a horrible mistake. That she hadn't seen the empty bottle. That he hadn't passed out from taking too many pills.

Laramie had texted her to let her know they'd admitted Landon to the hospital in stable condition, but Kelsey hadn't bothered to respond. While she was grateful he was okay, she didn't want to know any additional details.

It hurt too much.

The front door opened, and her mother stepped out carrying a mug of coffee in one hand and a baby monitor in the other. Her gray hair was matted on one side, and she offered a tired smile as she sank into the rocking chair beside Kelsey. She smoothed her faded house-coat over her bare legs then put the monitor on the wood slats between them.

"Did you get some sleep?" her mother asked.

"Not really." Kelsey looked away and sipped her coffee.

"I'm sure you don't want to hear this, but I think you made a mistake leaving Landon."

Anger flared in Kelsey's stomach. She stopped rocking. "Mom, you can't be serious."

Her mother reached over and covered Kelsey's hand with her own. "Listen, I know what you're thinking and feeling, because I've been there myself—"

"Then why are you giving me such terrible advice?"

"Because you need to stop blaming Landon. He's not your dad, and he won't treat you like your father did."

"Ha." Kelsey barked out a laugh. "Did he pay you to say that? Because he used the same argument with me."

"It's true. Your father made a lot of mistakes. We all have. Landon has wrestled with addiction and mismanaging his money, but I saw how he cared for Adeline and the way he looked at you, and that is not a man who's going to leave you."

"Right. Because I left him first."

Her mother pulled her hand away. "Is that really something to be proud of?"

"No, I meant that I left before he could cause Adeline or me any more pain."

Her mother's gaze bored into her. "You're feeling confident you made the right decision, then?"

Yes. No. She shifted in her chair.

"That's what I thought," her mother said softly. "Honey, I haven't done a good job of talking to you about my faith. I get all nervous and tongue-tied, worried I'll say the wrong thing or people will call me a hypocrite, but knowing the Lord and leaning on Him is the only thing that's carried me through the hard times."

More tears slid from Kelsey's eyes.

"We all mess up, and we all need grace. It took me a long time to even understand the concept. I've finally learned to accept that because God extends grace to me, I can do the same for others. There's so much freedom in living that way."

"That's great, but what does that have to do with me and Adeline?"

"I'm trying to say that you need to be gracious. For now, Adeline belongs with Landon, and when you're finished with the navy, the three of you can be together. You can build the life and the family I know you've always wanted. So don't let your stubborn pride keep you from all that God has for you. His plans are much better than yours."

Kelsey used the edge of the quilt to dab at her tears. "It's so hard for me to trust," she whispered. "I mean, look at me. After all these years, I still have issues because of my father. How could I possibly leave Adeline with Landon, knowing she's probably going to experience a similar hurt if she stays with him?"

"What if you're wrong? What if Landon's mistakes and shortcomings have set him up to be the ideal dad?"

"That's an enormous risk."

"Loving someone is often risky. Humans mess up all the time, but nothing is a surprise to the Lord. Landon is her father." Her mother's eyes filled with empathy. "You can't keep them from one another. That's not right."

"I'll be so far away," Kelsey insisted. "If something

goes wrong…" She couldn't bring herself to say the words out loud.

"What are you planning to do with Adeline when you go back to Hawaii? As much as Bill and I'd love to help, you know we can't take care of her. At least not right now."

Kelsey tipped her head back against the rocking chair. "We never made it to our appointment with the attorney, but depending on what he said, I figured I was going to have to ask someone in Landon's family to be Adeline's guardian. I can't take her with me to Hawaii, and I still have to file a new care plan. The childcare I need isn't available, especially when I deploy for dives."

Mom reached for her coffee. "I agree, that's too much stress and upheaval for a young child to tolerate."

Kelsey's heart fisted. Oh, her sweet precious girl. What was she going to do?

At the end of her folks' long driveway, a vehicle slowed then turned in at the entrance to the ranch. As the familiar white pickup truck moved toward them, Kelsey squeezed the armrest of the rocking chair.

"That's Landon," she said.

Her mother's smile stretched wide. "I knew he'd come."

The truck's engine rumbled, and the pungent aroma of exhaust floated toward the porch. Kelsey stared at him through the windshield. His gaze locked on hers, sending her heart into a free fall.

"I'd better go check on Bill. You two take as long as you need. I can take care of Adeline for a few minutes." Her mother quickly gathered the baby monitor and her coffee and hurried inside.

* * *

Once his eyes met Kelsey's through the windshield of his truck, he couldn't look away. He'd made it. Finally. *Thank You, Lord*, he prayed silently as he cut the engine then climbed out of the truck.

She stayed in the rocking chair on the porch, a faded quilt wrapped around her shoulders. Her hair was piled in that same messy bun she'd worn that stormy night she showed up on his porch. The night she'd walked back into his life and turned his whole world upside down with the news that he was a dad.

He walked toward her slowly, his heart thrumming. Her frigid gaze stopped him at the bottom of the steps. "Hey," he said, letting his gaze roam her face. "It's good to see you."

"Why are you here, Landon?"

Okay, a little exasperated—he could work with that. She obviously wasn't going to roll out the red carpet or offer him coffee and cinnamon rolls. Not that he blamed her for being suspicious. He deserved it.

"I came to see you and our daughter. I would've been here sooner. Yesterday, actually, but once I was discharged from the hospital, I had to meet with my sponsor and my counselor."

She kept staring at him, those gorgeous eyes boring right into him. He'd prayed several times on the long drive for the right words. For another shot at redemption, and that the Lord would soften her heart. Help her to trust him, trust that he could be the man that she and Adeline both needed.

"I'm glad you're getting some help."

Not exactly the response he'd hoped for, but he wouldn't let it stop him from saying everything he'd come to say. "Kelsey, I am sorry. After the fire at the silos, I was worn-out and hurting and afraid that we might've lost a huge portion of our harvest. And I had those pills hidden in my truck. Given my past behavior, I shouldn't have done anything that gave you a reason to suspect that I'd started using again. And I almost took them. But I—"

"Don't lie to me." Her voice crackled with raw emotion. "I found the empty bottle."

"I'm telling you the truth. I had the pills in my hand, and I planned on taking every single one. Except I realized that if I did, I'd be breaking my promise to you. Worse, I'd wreck any shot I had at a future with you and Adeline. So I went inside and flushed all of them, then passed out on the floor. I'm sure you must've been terrified when you found me, and I don't blame you for assuming the worst. I should've called you or sent a text and told you about the fire, because things might've been different. Again, I'm sorry, and I hope that you can forgive me."

"Wait." Her eyes narrowed. "Go back to the beginning. What fire?"

"I got a text alert in the middle of the night calling all volunteer firefighters to the silos out on Highway 22. A lot of farmers in the area store their grain there until it's ready to be transported to market. No one knows what happened exactly, but something ignited a fire. We tried our best to put it out." He stopped short of telling her about the rescue and the AED. That wasn't why he'd driven all this way. "Anyway, I'm not here to manipulate you with that story or try to justify my behavior. I'm sorry I hurt you. I'm in recovery, and with the Lord's help and support from my church, my family and friends, I promise that I will be the best man that I can be. You have my word that I'll keep trying to stay clean and sober."

"It's not that simple. I can't pretend none of this happened."

"I'm not asking you to pretend anything."

She twisted the edge of the quilt around her fingers. "Why should I believe you? Finding you facedown on the floor scared me to death. What if Adeline had been with you?"

"I'm grateful Adeline was safe with you. That doesn't change the facts, though. I was dehydrated. I didn't take the pills."

"I want to believe you. I do. But if I leave her with you and I'm on the other side of the world, how can I trust that you're going to keep her safe? That you're not going to be tempted to start using again?"

If?

Something that resembled hope zipped through his body. "Hold up. Does that mean you're thinking about letting me keep Adeline when you go back to Hawaii?"

"I was willing to consider it, especially when you said you were hiring an attorney and asking for primary parenting responsibility. Now I don't know what to do." She trapped her lip behind her teeth. "I thought about asking your sister or your parents or even Gage and Skye. Except they have busy lives and families and your sister's going to have a newborn soon. Your parents are lovely, but they don't want to be responsible for a young child."

She'd given him an inch. The door to the future he'd longed for eased open. And he was more than willing to seize the opportunity to convince her Adeline could stay with him. "My family, especially my parents, would be thrilled if Adeline's close by. You don't need to worry that I won't be able to handle being a single parent, because I will have plenty of help. In case you haven't noticed, people in Merritt's Crossing love to help. It's one of the many blessings of living there. That and Mrs. Wilkerson's peach cobbler."

Okay, so now he was jabbering like an idiot.

Her mouth tipped up in a half smile. "That cobbler was amazing. You're right about that."

"You know what else I'm right about?" He moved toward her and slowly climbed the porch until he stood next to her rocking chair.

"I'm sure you're going to tell me."

He reached for her hands then pulled her to her feet. "You're beautiful and talented, and Adeline is incredibly blessed to have you as her mother."

"Landon—"

He reached out and pressed his finger to her pink lips. "Let me finish, please. I am so sorry for everything I have done that has caused you pain. I hate that I left you alone in that hotel room, forcing you to figure out pregnancy and motherhood on your own. I'm sure I've scared you multiple times and probably made you cry gallons of tears. More than anything, I regret all the time I've missed with you and with Adeline."

Moisture shimmered in her eyes, and that tiny number eleven appeared between her brows.

"I love you, Kelsey Sinclair. Please forgive me." He cradled her face in his hands and caressed her cheekbones with his thumbs. His heart pounded as he waited for her to answer.

"You're forgiven," she finally whispered. "I love you, too." Her gaze dropped to his mouth.

"May I kiss you?"

"Please do."

He closed the distance between them and brushed his lips against hers. She tasted like coffee and smelled like lavender. Her body fit nicely against his, and holding her in his arms was the sweetest antidote to his heartache.

As the blanket dropped from her shoulders and she slid her arms around him then clutched fistfuls of his T-shirt, he deepened the kiss, showing her how much he loved her. How much he cared and how much he wanted to be with her.

A muffled screech and the sound of a palm slapping the window interrupted them.

Kelsey pulled away and rested her forehead against his. He sneaked a glance over her shoulder. Adeline stood at the living room window, grinning at them while she smacked her palm against the glass.

"Why don't you come inside and say hello to our daughter?"

"I thought you'd never ask."

Lacing her fingers through his, she led him into the house. Adeline squealed with excitement, then turned from the window and took her first tentative steps toward them.

"Oh my." Kelsey squeezed Landon's hand. "Look at her go."

"Come here, cutie pie." Landon opened his arms, and Adeline toddled into them. Her slobbery, toothy grin made his heart expand. He picked her up, then drew Kelsey into an embrace, sandwiching their baby girl in a gentle hug.

Now that she'd discovered how to walk, Adeline had zero interest in being held. She screeched and pushed against Landon's arms.

He chuckled then set her free. She toddled back toward the toys scattered across the living room floor.

Kelsey slid her arm around Landon's waist, and they stood together, staring at their beautiful little girl.

"Thank you." The warmth reflected in Kelsey's eyes nearly took him to his knees.

"For what?"

"Thank you for never giving up on me. On us."

"I'll be forever grateful that you had the courage to show up on my porch that night. Adeline and I are blessed to have you." He leaned down and brushed her lips with his own. "You've taught me that love is worth fighting for."

Epilogue

Two years later

Sunlight filtered through the trees and spilled across Gage and Skye's backyard, bathing everything in a buttery golden glow. Children giggled and hollered, romping around the grass and taking turns on the new tire swing Gage had suspended from a sturdy tree branch. Connor challenged Drew to a duel with a foam pool noodle, their exuberant yells punctuating the warm late-summer evening.

Kelsey stood on the deck, smiling as Landon set Adeline down and she immediately went after an inflated beach ball one of the other kids had left behind.

Drew offered a casual wave from the grill, where he was adding slices of cheese to the burgers cooking. Once upon a time, she'd have avoided a gathering like this. But ever since she'd married into the Chambers family in an intimate ceremony last winter, she'd looked forward to their casual get-togethers, especially when they included the Tomlinsons. Tonight, she'd brought a tray of deviled eggs and a pan of homemade brownies to add to the abundant spread of food filling the card table on the far side of the deck.

She gasped as Landon's broad hands slid around her waist. He nuzzled her neck, sending goose bumps dancing down her arms.

"Sorry, Mrs. Chambers," he murmured. "I'm having trouble keeping my hands to myself."

Kelsey covered his hands with her own, sighing as he kissed her below the ear.

She turned to face him, then looped her fingers behind his neck. "I have something to tell you. Something good, and I can't wait another second."

Landon slid his hands around her waist while his smoldering gaze searched her face. "Tell me."

"I'm pregnant."

His broad smile stretched wide. "When did you find out?"

"I took about four pregnancy tests, then I confirmed it with the doctor this afternoon. She found a heartbeat and estimated I'm about ten weeks along."

"Sweetheart, that's incredible." He leaned in and kissed her tenderly. "I'm so happy."

She pressed her palm against the golden stubble clinging to his jaw. When he deepened the kiss, a delicious shiver swirled through her.

One of the guys whistled, and Landon pulled away, then swept her into his arms and swung her around in a circle.

When he set her down, he turned and faced the backyard. "Hey, everybody, guess what?"

Their families circled up, shushed the kids, then swung expectant gazes their way.

"We're pregnant." He took Kelsey's hand in his and thrust them both into the air.

Landon's parents reached them first, hugging her then congratulating Landon.

The next few minutes were a blur of more hugs and handshakes and a few high fives from the little kids.

Adeline ran across the lawn toward them as fast as her little legs could carry her. At almost three years old, she had zero fear and constantly kept Kelsey on her toes.

"Hi, Mommy." She grinned and flung her body into Kelsey's legs.

"Hi, baby girl."

Kelsey tried to pick her up, but Landon got her first.

"I'm not your baby." Adeline pooched out her lower lip. "Me big."

"You are big," Landon agreed. "And you're going to be an amazing big sister."

"Sister?" Adeline's questioning blue eyes slid toward Kelsey.

"Yes, your mama has a baby growing in her tummy. One day, a long time from now, the baby will be born and you will be a big sister." Landon gently tapped the end of her nose with his finger.

She quirked her adorable little lips to one side. "How many wake ups?"

Kelsey laughed. "A lot of wake ups."

Landon pretended to count on his fingers. "More than two hundred."

Adeline heaved a dramatic sigh. "Can't wait that long."

Landon chuckled. "It does take a long time to grow a baby, but we'll be busy getting ready. Mom and I will need your help, because babies need a bunch of stuff."

Adeline pondered this, then she squirmed in Landon's arms. "Me get down."

"All right." Landon kissed her forehead and set her on the ground. She took off squealing and laughing as she tried to catch up with Connor, Charlotte, Macey, and Laramie and Jack's little boy, Sam. Gage and Skye's son, Theo, clung to the tire swing chains, giggling while Gage pushed him.

Connor had talked his cousins into a game of tag while the adults put the finishing touches on the meal and grabbed drinks.

Landon looped his arm around Kelsey's shoulders and pulled her against him. "I'm so happy with you."

She smiled up at him. "I'm so happy with you, too."

"We've had a couple detours along the way, but I wouldn't want any life other than the one we're building together."

She pressed up on her toes and kissed him again. "Thank you for giving me the family I've always wanted."

He brushed one more tender kiss to her lips before his mother politely cleared her throat. "Let's go, you two. We're ready to say the blessing."

They corralled the children and formed a circle in the yard beside the deck. Kelsey surveyed their group and silently thanked the Lord for bringing her into this community. Even if she had come dragging her feet, kicking and screaming.

It had been a long road finishing her commitment with the navy. She'd missed Landon and Adeline fiercely. Some days, she was so sad and lonely in Hawaii without them she could barely do her job. Landon and Adeline had come to visit her twice, and they met in California twice.

Once she separated from the navy, she'd moved back to Colorado and enrolled in nursing school right after they got married. Although this little one growing inside her was an unexpected surprise, she wasn't the least bit upset about having to change her future career plans. She'd finish nursing school before he or she was born. Even if she couldn't start working right away, she was content to let God's plans for her unfold one day at a time.

Because, like her mother had told her, God's plans for her were much better than anything she could come up with on her own.

* * * * *

If you enjoyed this story by Heidi McCahan, be sure to read her other romances set in Merritt's Crossing:

Their Baby Blessing
An Unexpected Arrangement

Available now from Love Inspired!

Dear Reader,

Have you ever faced a difficult situation that you desperately wanted to avoid? I find that in those hard seasons, I'm eager to skip ahead, as if it's possible to outrun my circumstances. I tend to cling to the illusion that I'm in control.

I faced a challenging turn of events while I was writing this book. I wanted to skip the hard stuff, but I couldn't. God had things to show me in the middle of a difficult season, and while I longed for a different outcome, He equipped me to trust in Him. I've been reminded often that He is our hope and the One we can run to, no matter the circumstances.

Thank you, readers, for supporting Christian fiction and telling your friends how much you enjoy our books. I'd love to connect with you. You can find me online: www.facebook.com/heidimccahan, www.heidimccahan.com or www.instagram.com/heidimccahan.author. For news about book releases and sales, sign up for my author newsletter: www.subscribepage.com/heidimccahan-newoptin.

Until next time,
Heidi

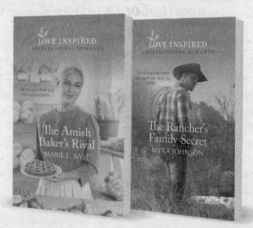

COMING NEXT MONTH FROM
Love Inspired

SNOWBOUND WITH THE AMISH BACHELOR
Redemption's Amish Legacies • by Patricia Johns
When social worker Grace Schweitzer arrives at the Hochstetler family farm to pick up an abandoned baby, a blizzard leaves her stranded. Grace has no plans to return to the Amish life she left behind, but soon she's losing her heart to bachelor Ben Hochstetler *and* the faith she once held dear.

HIS AMISH WIFE'S HIDDEN PAST
by Mindy Steele
Englischer Hannah Raber will do anything to protect her children when they are sent into witness protection—even marry her late husband's brother. But learning to be an Amish wife to Daniel is an adjustment. Can these strangers from different worlds turn a convenient marriage into a forever love?

FINDING A CHRISTMAS HOME
Rescue Haven • by Lee Tobin McClain
As the new guardian to her twin nieces, Hannah Antonicelli is determined to keep her promise to her late sister—that she'll never reveal the identity of their father. But when the twins' uncle, Luke Hutchenson, is hired as a handyman at her job and begins to bond with the little girls, keeping the secret isn't easy...

HER HOLIDAY SECRET
Cowboys of Diamondback Ranch • by Jolene Navarro
As a pregnant teen, Catalina Wimberly sacrificed everything to protect Andres Sanchez's future. Now she's temporarily back in town to tell him he's a father. There's no doubt he'll love their five-year-old daughter, but will he ever be able to forgive Catalina?

A SAFE PLACE FOR CHRISTMAS
by Lisa Carter
When Christmas tree farmer Luke Morgan finds his childhood friend Shayla Coggins and her baby in their broken-down car during a snowstorm, he offers them a place to stay for the holidays. But while her son draws the pair together, Shayla's dark secret threatens to end their budding romance.

THE FAMILY HE NEEDS
by Lorraine Beatty
From the moment Joy Duncan goes to work for reclusive Simon Baker, their relationship is contentious—despite his instant bond with her little boy. But Joy begins to wonder if there's more to Simon beneath his pain and anger. Could this hurting widower be the father and husband her little family needs?

LOOK FOR THESE AND OTHER LOVE INSPIRED BOOKS WHEREVER BOOKS ARE SOLD, INCLUDING MOST BOOKSTORES, SUPERMARKETS, DISCOUNT STORES AND DRUGSTORES.

LICNM0921

SPECIAL EXCERPT FROM

LOVE INSPIRED
INSPIRATIONAL ROMANCE

*Newly guardian to her twin nieces, Hannah Antonicelli
is determined to keep her last promise to her late
sister—that she'll never reveal the identity of their
father. But when Luke Hutchenson is hired as a
handyman at her work and begins to bond with the little
girls, hiding that he's their uncle isn't easy...*

Read on for a sneak peek at
Finding a Christmas Home *by Lee Tobin McClain!*

On Wednesday after work, Hannah drove toward home, the
twins in the back seat, and tried not to be nervous that Luke
was in the front seat beside her.

"I really appreciate this," he said. His car hadn't started this
morning, and he'd walked the three miles to Rescue Haven.

Of course, Hannah had insisted on driving him home. What
else could she do? It was cold outside, spitting snow, and he
was her next-door neighbor.

"I hate to ask another favor," he said, "but could you stop by
Pasquale's Pizza on the way?"

"No problem." She took a left and drove the two blocks to
the only nonchain pizza place in Bethlehem Springs.

He jumped out, and she turned back to check on the twins,
trying not to watch Luke as he headed into the shop. He was
good-looking, of course. Kind, appreciative and strong. And he
had the slightest swagger in his walk that was masculine and
appealing.

But he was also about to go visit his brother, Bobby, if he kept his promise to his ailing father. And when she'd heard about that visit, it had been a wake-up call: she shouldn't get too close with him. The fewer chances she had to spill the beans about Bobby being the twins' father, the better.

He came out of the pizza shop quickly—he must have called ahead—carrying a big flat box and a white bag. What would it be like if this was a family scenario, if they were Mom and Dad and kids, stopping for takeout on the way home from work?

She couldn't help it. Her chest filled with longing.

He climbed into her small car, juggling the large flat box to make it fit without encroaching on the gearshift.

She had to laugh at the size of his meal. "Hungry?"

"Are you?" He opened the box a little, and the rich, garlicky fragrance of Pasquale's special sauce filled the car.

Her stomach growled, loudly.

"Pee-zah!" Addie shouted from the back seat.

"Peez!" Emmy added, almost as loud.

"That's just cruel," she said as she pulled the car back onto the road and steered toward Luke's place. "You're tempting us. I may have to order some when I get these girls home."

"No, you won't," he said. "This is for all of us. The least I can do is feed you, after you drove me around."

Her stomach gave a little leap, and not just about the prospect of pizza. Why was he inviting her to have dinner with him? Was there an ulterior motive? And if there was, would she mind?

Don't miss
Finding a Christmas Home *by Lee Tobin McClain,*
available October 2021 wherever
Love Inspired books and ebooks are sold.

LoveInspired.com

LIEXP0921

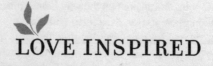